图书在版编目（CIP）数据

论语意解／（春秋）孔丘著；刘伟见译．－北京：线装书局，2005.4
ISBN7－80106－423－2
Ⅰ.论… Ⅱ.①孔…②刘… Ⅲ.①儒家②论语—译文—汉、英 Ⅳ.B222.2
中国版本图书馆CIP数据核字（2005）第028539号

论语意解

译　　者	刘伟见
责任编辑	李　莉
策　　划	集雅山房
出版发行	线装书局
地　　址	北京西城区鼓楼西大街41号
印　　刷	扬州市邗江古籍印刷厂
版　　次	2005年5月第1版第1次印刷
印　　数	1——1000
书　　号	ISBN7－80106－423－2
定　　价	1300元

ISBN 7-80106-4232
9787801064233

论语意解

刘伟见 译

线装书局

《论语》译序

犹记得十六年前刚刚接触《论语》时，家中前辈说每日涵泳一二句，便觉当日浮想联翩，不能再多读。年少的我当时觉得自己日读数十万字，每日日记三四千言，如此薄的《论语》不就是一时半会儿的事吗？

十六年里，那套朱子注的《四书》伴我从初中到高中，从离开家乡那个小山城到北京，在求学与蛰居北大的七八年里，直至今天成为一个出版人，我一直反复在读《论语》。这可能是值得一辈子读的书。因为，他已经融入到我们民族的心理与个性中去了。甚至在某种程度上也改造了我的个性。

我很欣赏迦达默尔所说的，我们每个人是被抛入了一种文化处境，我们不可避免地要受传统视角与风格的制约。所以，我对这么一份中华民族最重要的传统的核心文献之一的文本，充满了兴趣。应当说，因为略有家学的缘故，我基本上将我在学校所受的对于这本书的结论性观点归纳到了另一个文化视角；即作为我在阅读与累积西方文化的过程中的某种延续。简言之，中国的就是中国的。它不太适合别的尺度的裁剪。但这并不意味着两种文化之间缺乏共通性，恰恰相反，在全球化日益加剧的今天，《论语》的世界性先于其民族性得到了彰显。

所以当线装书局的李莉编辑邀请我作为线装本的《论语意解》的作者时，我欣然承应而又惶恐久之。因为时

间之短与我学问之浅深恐见笑于大方之家。尽管在多年的阅读与体认中我有一些不同于前人之见。有一点需要注意的是，我们现代汉语所传达的一些意思较之古代汉语可能存在歧义。比如关于"人不知而不愠，不亦君子乎"几乎每一本国内翻译的白话论语都翻译为"人家不了解我，我却不生气，不也是君子吗"，单从字面理解，可能会有这样的疑问，人们之间不了解的多了，要生气生得过来吗？如果你是一个土木工程师，一个音乐家可能不了解你，你会因此而生气？你不生气就表明你有教养？如果通读《论语》，与其他章节参酌互证，比如，"不患不己知，求为可知也"，才知道说的是别人不了解你的学问、道德，甚至误解你，你并不因此而生气。这才是君子的风范。又如"唯仁者能好人，能恶人"通行的译本是"只有仁人能喜欢人，能厌恶人"。我们可能要问，别人就不能喜欢人与厌恶人吗，这是每个人的权利呀。其实细推之，才知原意是只有仁人能更好地代表一种欢喜和厌恶他人的标准。所以，如何从现代汉语角度更准确表达古人的原意，可能是格外需要注意的问题。这也许是文字学家们的常识，但对喜欢深究义理的人来说，很容易犯自己理解了，就以为别人也理解了的毛病。

匆匆为之，错漏必不少，祈请读者指正。

是为序。

刘伟见

2005年3月21日 于一得斋

Preface to the Interpretation of the Analects of Confucius

Still remember that when I was going to read the Analects 16 years ago, the older generation in my family told me if I read aloud just a few lines of the Analects each day, I would feel having so many imaginations one after another in my mind that I could not read it any more in that very day. So young as I was at that time, I thought since I could read hundreds thousand words a day, and I could write down three or four thousand words in my diary everyday, I could finish reading such thin Analects in a short time,

The Four Books, annotated by Zhu Zi, has accompanied me for 16 years, from my junior middle school to my senior middle school, and from I being away from home, located in a small mountain city, to Beijing, then together with me when I studied in the Peking University for seven or eight years, up to now I becoming a publisher. I have repeatedly read the Analects all along, which is a work worthy of being read all one's life, I think, because this book has incorporated into the psychology and individual character of our nations. Even to a certain extent this book also reforms my personality.

I appreciate very much the word that Hans-Georg Gadamer said that each one of us was thrown into a kind of cultural situation, in which we were unavoidably restricted by the conventional visual angle and style. So I am full of interest in the Analects which is one of the leading literatures with the most important tradition of China. Because somewhat the Analects has intellectual background of the family, I basically put the conclusion point of view about this book, which I received in the university, under the cultural angle of view. That is I have it as a certain kind of continuity in the duration of my reading the western culture and accumulating the concerned knowledge. In short, a Chinese thing is exactly Chinese, it is unsuitable to be transformed with another criterion. But this does not mean that there is short of something applicable to two kinds of cultures. Just the opposite, nowadays when the globalization grows intensive, one of Analects' characters of belonging to the whole world is more evident than its national character.

So when Ms. Li Li, the editor of the Publishing House of the Thread-bound Books, invited me to be the author of the thread-bound-edition Analects (Chinese and English), I joyfully agreed. But for a somewhat long time I also have been very much feared of being laughed at by the experts due to the short time for me to finish the interpretation and my comparatively superficial knowledge as well although by my so many years' reading and realizing I have some views different from the predecessors. There is one worthy of attention that some different meanings exist between modern Chinese and ancient Chinese when they express some ideas. For example, with regard to a sentence in the Analects, almost all its interpretations in the written form of modern Chinese are "I am not angry though other people don't understand me. So I am a man of noble character". But from the literal meaning, we may think that in fact there are too many cases of not understanding people for a man to get angry if he is angry for such matter. And if you are a civil engineering, a musician probably doesn't understand you. Will you then be angry for it? Can it indicate that you are a cultured man if you don'Žt get angry? If you read over the Analects, and you consider and prove with other chapters and sections of the work, we will know that the meaning of the above-mentioned sentence is actually that only this is the style of a man of noble character that facing other people not knowing about your knowledge and morals, even they misunderstanding you, you don't get angry. Another example is that the general interpretation of a sentence in the Analects is that only merciful people can like and detest people. Can't other people do? This is a question we will possibly put forward because liking and detesting people is the right of everyone. In fact if we make a careful inference, we can know that the meaning of the sentence should be

Preface to the Interpretation of the Analects of Confucius

Still remember that when I was going to read the Analects 16 years ago, the older generation in my family told me if I read aloud just a few lines of the Analects each day, I would feel having so many imaginations one after another in my mind that I could not read it any more in that very day. So young as I was at that time, I thought since I could read hundreds thousand words a day, and I could write down three or four thousand words in my diary everyday, I could finish reading such thin Analects in a short time.

The Four Books, annotated by Zhu Zi, has accompanied me for 16 years from my junior middle school to my senior middle school, and from I being away from home, located in a small mountain city, to Beijing, then together with me when I studied in the Peking University for seven or eight years, up to now I becoming a publisher. I have repeatedly read the Analects all along, which is a work worthy of being read all one's life, I think, because this book has incorporated into the psychology and individual character of our nations. Even to a certain extent this book also reforms my personality.

I appreciate very much the word that Hans-Georg Gadamer said that each one of us was thrown into a kind of cultural situation, in which we were unavoidably restricted by the conventional visual angle and style. So I am full of interest in the Analects, which is one of the leading literatures with the most important tradition of China. Because somewhat the Analects has intellectual background of the family, I basically put the conclusion point of view about this book, which I received in the university, under the cultural angle of view. That is I have it as a certain kind of continuity in the duration of my reading the western culture and accumulating the concerned knowledge. In short, a Chinese thing is exactly Chinese, it is unsuitable to be transformed with another criterion. But this does not mean

that there is short of something applicable to two kinds of cultures. Just the opposite, nowadays when the globalization grows intensive, one of Analects characters of belonging to the whole world is more evident than its national character.

So when Ms. Li Ti, the editor of the Publishing House of the Thread-bound Books, invited me to be the author of the thread-bound-edition Analects (Chinese and English), I joyfully agreed. But for a somewhat long time I also have been very much feared of being laughed at by the experts due to the short time for me to finish the interpretation and my comparatively superficial knowledge as well although by my so many years' reading and realizing I have some views different from the predecessors. There is one worthy of attention that some different meanings exist between modern Chinese and ancient Chinese when they express some ideas. For example with regard to a sentence in the Analects, almost all its interpretations in the written form of modern Chinese are "I am not angry though other people don't understand me. So I am a man of noble character." But from the literal meaning, we may think that in fact there are too many cases of not understanding people for a man to get angry if he is angry for such matter. And if you are a civil engineering, a musician probably doesn't understand you. Will you then be angry for it? Can reinidioterthat you are a cultured man if you don't get angry? If you read over the Analects, and you consider and prove with other chapters and sections of the work, we will know that the meaning of the above-mentioned sentence is actually that only this is the style of a man of noble character that facing other people not knowing about your knowledge and morals, even they misunderstanding you, you don't get angry. Another example is that the general interpretation of a sentence in the Analects is that the only merciful people can like and detest people. Can't other people do? This is a question we will possibly put forward because liking and detesting people is the right of everyone. In fact if we make a careful inference, we can know that the meaning of the sentence should be the merciful man can better represent a kind of standard for liking and detesting people. So how to more precisely express, from the angle of the modern Chinese, the original meaning of the ancient people is possibly a question especially needing our attention. Perhaps this is probably the general knowledge of the expert in philology. But for the people who like to seriously go into the principle on word's meaning, they easily have the defect that in their opinion as long as they themselves understand, other people will understand too.

Hereby sincerely hope your readers don't hesitate to criticize us for our inadequacies and errors due to our hurry in the interpretation.

Weijian, Liu
Writing in the Yi De Study
March 21, 2005

the merciful man can better represent a kind of standard for liking and detesting people. So how to more precisely express, from the angle of the modern Chinese, the original meaning of the ancient people is possibly a question especially needing our attention. Perhaps this is probably the general knowledge of the expert in philology. But for the people who like to seriously go into the principle on word's meaning, they easily have the defect that in their opinion as long as they themselves understand, other people will understand too.

Hereby sincerely hope your readers don't hesitate to criticize us for our inadequacies and errors due to our hurry in the interpretation.

Weijian, Lü
Writing in the Yi De Study
March 21, 2005

目 录 Contents

1. 学而篇第一
   On Learning .... 一六
2. 为政篇第二
   On Governing .... 三八
3. 八佾篇第三
   On Ritural .... 六七
4. 里仁篇第四
   On Virtue .... 八八
5. 公冶长篇第五
   Talking about the Important People .... 一一八
6. 雍也篇第六
   What Confucius and his Students said .... 一四七
7. 述而篇第七
   About Confucius Being Modest .... 一八〇
8. 泰伯篇第八
   Confucius and Zengzi Talking the Ancient People ...... 二〇一
9. 子罕篇第九
   Encourage People to study hard .... 二二〇
10. 乡党篇第十
    On the Habit of Confucius .... 二五八
11. 先进篇第十一
    Remark about Confucius' Students .... 二八九
12. 颜渊篇第十二
    On How to Have Charity in the Heart .... 三一四
13. 子路篇第十三
    Confucius Teaching His Students How to Be a Good Person ...... 三四三
14. 宪问篇第十四
    Confucius And His Students Talking about the Way of Being a Gentleman ... 三八八

15. 卫灵公篇第十五
    Confucius And His Students Talking about How to Govern the State ..... 四二一
16. 季氏篇第十六
    Confucius Talking about How a Gentleman Act .... 四四二
17. 阳货篇第十七
    On Governing the State According to Ritural .... 四七一
18. 微子篇第十八
    The Attitude Towards the world .... 四八八
19. 子张篇第十九
    The Students' Respect for Confucius .... 五一一
20. 尧约篇第二十
    About What Yao Said .... 五二〇

论语意解

目录 Contents

1. 学而篇第一
On Learning .... 六

2. 为政篇第二
On Governing .... 二八

3. 八佾篇第三
On Ritual .... 六七

4. 里仁篇第四
On Virtue .... 八八

5. 公冶长篇第五
Talking about the Important People .... 八一

6. 雍也篇第六
What Confucius and his Students said .... 一四

7. 述而篇第七
About Confucius Being Modest .... 一八〇

8. 泰伯篇第八
Confucius and Zengzi Talking the Ancient People .... 一〇

9. 子罕篇第九
Encourage People to study hard .... 一〇三

10. 乡党篇第十
On the Habit of Confucius .... 一一五

11. 先进篇第十一
Remark about Confucius' Students .... 一二八

12. 颜渊篇第十二
On How to Have Charity in the Heart .... 一四

13. 子路篇第十三
Confucius Teaching His Students How to Be a Good Person .... 一三

14. 宪问篇第十四
Confucius And His Students Talking about the Way of Being a Gentleman .... 一三八

15. 卫灵公篇第十五
Confucius And His Students Talking about How to Govern the State .... 一四

16. 季氏篇第十六
Confucius Talking about How a Gentleman Act .... 一四

17. 阳货篇第十七
On Governing the State According to Ritual .... 一七

18. 微子篇第十八
The Attitude Towards the world .... 一四八

19. 子张篇第十九
The Students' Respect for Confucius .... 一五

20. 尧曰篇第二十
About What Yao Said .... 一五〇

学而篇第一（共十六章）

On Learning

1.1

子曰[1]："学而时习之，不亦说乎[2]！有朋自远方来，不亦乐乎！人不知而不愠[3]，不亦君子乎[4]！"

【中译文】

孔子说："学习了知识而时常付诸于实践，不也愉快吗！有朋友从远方来相聚，不也快乐吗！别人不了解我的学问与道德，我并不烦恼怨恨，不也是君子的风范吗！"

【注释】

1 子：古人对有地位、有学问、有道德修养的人，尊称为"子"。这里是尊称孔子。

2 说（yuè）：同"悦"，高兴，喜悦。

3 愠（yùn）：怨恨，烦恼。

4 君子：含义有二：其一，有道德修养的人。其二，官职地位高的人。这里采用第一种含义。

【英译文】

The Master (Confucius) said, to learn and at due times to review what one has learnt, is not that a pleasure? That friends should come to one from afar,

---

is not that delightful? To remain unsoured even though one's merits are unrecognised by others, is not that what is expected of a gentleman?

1.2

有子曰[1]："其为人也孝弟[2]，而好犯上者，鲜矣[3]；不好犯上，而好作乱者，未之有也。君子务本，本立而道生。孝弟也者，其为仁之本与[4]。"

【中译文】

有子说，"做人，孝顺父母，尊敬兄长，而喜好冒犯长辈和上司的情形，是很少见的；不喜好冒犯长辈和上司，而喜欢造反作乱的人，是没有的。君子要在根本上下工夫，根本确立了，修齐治平的原则就产生了。所谓'孝''悌'，就是'仁'的根本吧。"

【注释】

1 有子：鲁国人，姓有，名若，字子有。孔子的弟子。比孔子小三十三岁，生于公元前518年，卒年不详。另说，比孔子小十三岁。后世，有若的弟子也尊称有若为"子"，故称"有子"。

2 弟（tì）：同"悌"。弟弟善事兄长，称"悌"。

3 鲜（xiǎn）：少。

4 与：同"欤"。语气词。

【英译文】

You Zi said, Those who behave well towards their parents and elder brothers,

论语意解

论语

学而篇第一 （共十六章）
On Learning

1.1

子曰："学而时习之，不亦说乎？有朋自远方来，不亦乐乎？人不知而不愠，不亦君子乎？"

【中译文】

孔子说："学习了知识而时常去实践，不也愉快吗？有朋友从远方来相聚，不也快乐吗？别人不了解我的学问志趣，我并不烦恼怨恨，不也是君子的风范吗？"

【注释】

1 子：古人对有道德、有学问，有道德修养的人，尊称"子"。这里是尊称孔子。

2 说（yuè）：同"悦"，高兴，喜悦。

3 愠（yùn）：恼恨，怨恨。

4 君子：含义有二：其一，有道德修养的人。这里采用第一种含义。其二，旧时地位高的人。

【英译文】

The Master (Confucius) said, to learn and at due times to review what one has learnt, is not that a pleasure? That friends should come to one from afar, is not that delightful? To remain unsoured even though one's merits are unrecognised by others, is not that what is expected of a gentleman?

1.2

有子曰："其为人也孝弟，而好犯上者，鲜矣；不好犯上，而好作乱者，未之有也。君子务本，本立而道生。孝弟也者，其为仁之本与。"

【中译文】

有子说："做人，孝顺父母，敬爱兄长，而喜欢冒犯和触犯上司的，是很少见的；不喜欢冒犯和触犯上司，而喜欢造反作乱的人，是没有的。君子要致力于根本的工夫，根本确立了，修养治平的原则便产生了。所以说，孝、悌，就是'仁'的根本吧。"

【注释】

1 有子：曾国人，姓有，名若，字子有，孔子的弟子。比孔子小三十三岁，生于公元前518年，卒年不详。另说，比孔子小十三岁。后也，有若的弟弟子也尊称有若为"子"。故称"有子"。

2 弟（tì）：同"悌"，弟弟善事兄长。后"弟"。

3 鲜（xiǎn）：少。

4 与：同"欤"，语气词。

【英译文】

You Zi said, Those who behave well towards their parents and elder brothers.

事情，是否尽心竭力了？和朋友交往，是否真诚讲信用？对老师所传授的知识，是否自己实践了？"

【注释】

1 曾（zēng）子：姓曾，名参（shēn）字子舆。曾皙孔子。鲁国南武城（在今山东省枣庄市附近）人。孔子的弟子。比孔子小四十六岁，生于公元前505年，卒于公元前435年。其弟子也尊称曾参为"子"。

2 省（xǐng）：反省、自我检讨。

3 传：老师传授的知识、学问。孔子教学，有"六艺"：礼、乐、射、御、书、数。

【英译文】

Zeng zi said, Every day I examine myself on these three points: in acting on behalf of others, have I always been loyal to their interests? In intercourse with my friends, have I always been true to my word? Have I practiced what I was taught?

1.5

子曰："道千乘之国[1]，敬事而信，节用而爱人，使民以时[2]。"

【中译文】

孔子说："治理拥有千辆兵车的诸侯国，要尽心尽力于政事、取信于民；节约财政开支，又爱护部下和百姓；差使百姓一定要选择在农闲时进行。"

论语意解

四三

---

seldom show a disposition to resist the authority of their superiors. And as for such men starting a revolution, no instance of it has ever occurred. It is upon the fundamental that a gentleman works. When that is firmly set up, the Way grows. And surely proper behaviour towards parents and elder brothers is the fundamental of Goodness?

1.3

子曰："巧言令色[1]，鲜矣仁。"

【中译文】

孔子说："满口花言巧语，表面和顺谦恭，这种人是很少有仁德的。"

【注释】

1 令色：面色和善。这里指以恭维的态度讨好别人。

【英译文】

The Master (Confucius) said, 'Clever talk and a pretentious manner' have little to do with benevolence.

1.4

曾子曰[1]："吾日三省吾身[2]：为人谋而不忠乎？与朋友交而不信乎？传不习乎[3]？"

【中译文】

曾子说："我每天多次反省自检。为别人出主意做

The Master (Confucius) said, 'Clever talk and a pretentious manner have seldom to do with stuff.'

1.5

子曰："道千乘之国[1]，敬事而信，节用而爱人，使民以时[2]。"

【注释】

1 道：同"导"。领导，治理。乘（shèng）：古代称四匹马拉的一辆车为"一乘"。古代军队使用兵车，每辆兵车用四匹马拉，车上有身着盔甲的士兵三人，车下跟随有步兵七十二人，另有相应的后勤人员二十五人，因此，所谓"一乘"的实际兵力就是一百人，并非单指四匹马拉一辆车。按规定，"八百家出车一乘"。古代衡量一个诸侯国的大小强弱，就是看它拥有多少兵车，所谓"千乘之国"，"万乘之尊"。

2 杨伯峻《论语译注》：古代以农业为主，"使民以时"即是《孟子·梁惠王》上的"不违农时"。

【英译文】

The Master (Confucius) said, A country of a thousand war-chariots cannot be administered unless the ruler attends strictly to business, punctually observes his promises, is economical in expenditure, shows affection towards his subjects in general, and uses the labour of the peasantry only at the proper times of year.

1.6

子曰："弟子[1]，入则孝，出则弟[2]，谨而信，泛爱众而亲仁。行有馀力，则以学文。"

论语意解

六五

【中译文】

孔子说："年轻人，在家要孝顺父母，在外面要尊敬长辈，做人言行要谨慎而注重信用，博爱大众，亲近有仁德的人。如果做了这些还有余力，就要用来学习各种文化知识。"

【注释】

1 弟子：其含义有二：第一学生；第二年纪小的人。此处为第二种。
2 出：外出，出门。一说，离开自己住的房屋。

【英译文】

The Master (Confucius) said, A young man should behave well to his parents at home and to his elders abroad, He should be cautious in giving promises and punctual in keeping them, He should have kindly feelings towards everyone, but seek the intimacy of the Good. If, when all that is done, he has any energy to spare, then let him study literary culture.

1.7

子夏曰[1]："贤贤易色[2]；事父母，能竭其力；事君，能致其身[3]；与朋友交，言而有信。虽曰未学，吾必谓之学矣。"

【中译文】

子夏说："注重贤德甚于注重外表；事奉父母，能

论语

【中译文】

孔子说:"年轻人,在家要孝顺父母,在外则要尊敬长辈,做人言行要谨慎而讲重信用,博爱大众,亲近有仁德的人。如果做了这些还有余力,就要用来学习各种文化知识。"

【注释】

1. 弟子:其名义有二:第一,学生;第二,年纪小的人。此处取第二种。
2. 出:外出。出门:一说,离开自己住的居室。

【英译文】

The Master (Confucius) said, A young man should behave well to his parents at home and to his elders abroad. He should be cautious in giving promises and punctual in keeping them. He should have kindly feelings towards everyone, but seek the intimacy of the Good. If, when all that is done, he has any energy to spare, then let him study literary culture.

1.7

子夏曰:"贤贤易色;事父母,能竭其力;事君,能致其身;与朋友交,言而有信。虽曰未学,吾必谓之学矣。"

【中译文】

子夏说:"尊重贤能甚于迷重女色;奉养父母,能

六五

1.5

子曰:"道千乘¹之国²,人则寡,出则弟,谨而信,泛爱众而亲仁。行有余力,则以学文。"

【注释】

1. 道:同"导",治理。乘(shèng):古代称四匹马拉的一辆车。古代军队使用兵车,每辆用四匹马拉,车上有甲士三人,车下跟随有步卒七十二人,另有相应的后勤人员二十五人,并非单带四匹马拉一辆车。其规定是一辆车出"一乘"。古代衡量一个国家国力大小强弱,是看能出多少兵车,所谓"千乘之国","万乘之尊"。
2. 杨伯峻《论语译注》:古代以农业为主,"使民以时",即是《孟子·梁惠王》上的"不违农时"。

【英译文】

The Master (Confucius) said, A country of a thousand war-chariots cannot be administered unless the ruler attends strictly to business, punctually observes his promises, is economical in expenditure, shows affection towards his subjects in general, and uses the labour of the peasantry only at the proper times of year.

1.6

识就不巩固。做人要以忠诚、信用为主。不要去结交仁德比自己差的人做朋友。如果有了过错，就不要害怕改正。"

【注释】

1 固：巩固，牢固。

2 无：同"毋"。不要。友：做动词用。交朋友。

3 过：错误，过失。惮（dàn）：怕。

【英译文】

The Master (Confucius) said, If a gentleman is frivolous, he will lose the respect of his inferiors and lack firm ground upon which he can build up his education. First and foremost he must learn to be faithful to his superiors and to keep promises, He should not make friends with his in feriors. And if he finds he has made a mistake, then he must not be afraid of correcting it.

1.9

曾子曰："慎终[1]，追远[2]，民德归厚矣。"

【中译文】

曾子说："要慎重地办理好父母的丧事，虔诚地追祭祖先，这样，人民的道德就会归复淳厚。"

【注释】

1 终：寿终，指父母去世。

2 远：远祖，祖先。

竭尽全力；事奉君王，能奋不顾身；和朋友交往，能说到做到。这样的人即使自称未学，我也认为他学得很好了。"

【注释】

1 子夏：姓卜，名商，字子夏。孔子的弟子。比孔子小四十四岁，生于公元前 507 年，卒年不详。

2 贤贤：第一个"贤"做动词用，表示敬重，尊崇；第二个"贤"是名词，即"圣贤"的"贤"，指有道德有学问的高尚的人。易：轻视，不看重。一说"易"释为"移"，移好色之心而好贤德。

3 致：做出奉献。

【英译文】

Zi Xia said, a man who Treats his betters as betters, wears an air of respect, who into serving father and mother knows how to put his whole strength, who in the service of his prince will lay down his life, who in intercourse with friends is true to his word though he is said to be uneducated? would certainly call him an educated man.

1.8

子曰："君子不重则不威，学则不固[1]。主忠信。无友不如己者[2]。过则勿惮改[3]。"

【中译文】

孔子说："君子不厚重，就没有威严，所学习的知

论语

【英译文】

The Master (Confucius) said, If a gentleman is frivolous, he will lose the respect of his inferiors and lack firm ground upon which he can build up his education. First and foremost he must learn to be faithful to his superiors and to keep promises. He should not make friends with his inferiors. And if he finds he has made a mistake, then he must not be afraid of correcting it.

1.9

【英译文】

Zi xia said, a man who Treats his betters as betters, wears an air of respect, who into serving father and mother knows how to put his whole strength, who in the service of his prince will lay down his life, who in intercourse with friends is true to his word though he is said to be uneducated would certainly call him an educated man.

1.8

【英译文】

　Zeng zi said, When proper respect towards the dead is shown at the End and continued after they are far away the moralforce (te) of a people has reached its highest point.

1.10

　　子禽问于子贡曰¹："夫子至于是邦也²，必闻其政，求之与，抑与之与³？"子贡曰："夫子温、良、恭、俭、让以得之。夫子之求之也，其诸异乎人之求之与⁴？"

【中译文】

　　子禽问子贡："老师每到一个诸侯国，一定能了解那一国的政事，是他自己主动询问别人，还是别人主动告诉他的呢？"子贡说："老师是靠温和、恳切、恭敬、节制、谦让的方式来了解政事的。与别人求得的方法不相同吧？"

【注释】

1　子禽：姓陈，名亢(kàng)，字子禽。一说，即原亢。陈国人。孔子的弟子（一说，不是孔子的弟子）。
　　子贡：姓端木，名赐，字子贡。卫国人，孔子的弟子。比孔子小三十一岁，生于公元前520年，卒年不详。
2　夫子：孔子的弟子敬称孔子。邦：诸候国。

3　抑与之与："抑"，连词，表示选择，"还是……"。"与之"，给予。最后的"与"，同"欤"，语气词。
4　其诸：也许，大概。

【英译文】

　Zi Qin said to Zi Gong, When our Master arrives in a fresh country he always manages to find out about its policy. Does he do this by asking questions, or do people tell him of their own accord? Zi Gong said, Our Master gets things by being cordial, frank, courteous, temperate, deferential. That is our Master's way of enquiring-a very different matter, certainly, from the way in which enquiries are generally made.

1.11

　　子曰："父在，观其志；父没，观其行，三年无改于父之道¹，可谓孝矣。"

【中译文】

　　孔子说："父亲在世，要看他的志向；父亲死后，要考察他的行为，如果三年的行为都不改变，父道如在眼前，这样的人可以说是做到了孝。"

【注释】

1　三年：按照周礼，父亲死后，儿子要守孝三年。这里也可指一段较长的时间，或多年以后。此处指父死三年，子当父不在如在。旧释多泥于后一句，未与

语音意翻

3 仰之弥高："仰"，抬头看；"弥"，更加；"高"，高大。

4 其右：此指"大道"。

【英译文】

Zi Qin said to Zi Gong, When our Master arrives in a fresh country he always manages to find out about its policy. Does he do this by asking questions, or do people tell him of their own accord? Zi Gong said, Our Master gets things by being cordial, frank, courteous, temperate, deferential. That is our Master's way of enquiring—a very different matter; certainly, from the way in which enquiries are generally made.

1.11

子曰："父在，观其志；父没，观其行；三年无改于父之道，可谓孝矣。"

【中译文】

孔子说："父亲在世时，要观察他的志向；父亲死后，要考察他的行为。如果三年的行为都不改变，又遵循处世原则——这样的人才可以被称作了孝了。"

【注释】

1. 在事：根据错乱。父亲死后，儿子要学守孝三年。没有：去世。道：一般长的原则，或者年的行为，此处是指父亲的行为。"三年无改父之道一句"：未见。

1.10

子禽问于子贡曰："夫子至于是邦也，必闻其政，求之与，抑与之与？"子贡曰："夫子温、良、恭、俭、让以得之。夫子之求之也，其诸异乎人之求之与？"

【中译文】

子禽问子贡：老师每到一个国家来，一定能了解到那一国的政事。是他自己主动询问的，还是别人告诉他的呢？"子贡说："老师是靠温和、善良、恭敬、节俭、谦让的品德来了解到事情的。与别人求得的方法不是不相同吗？

【注释】

1. 子禽：陈亢。亢(kāng)，字子禽。陈国人。字子亢的孔子弟子。子贡：姓端木，名赐，字子贡，卫国人，孔子的弟子，年纪比孔子小三十一岁，生于公元前520年，卒年不详。

2. 夫子：孔子死后孔子弟子尊孔子，称：夫子。

【英译文】

Zeng zi said, When proper respect towards the dead is shown at the End and continued after they are far away the moral force (te) of a people has reached its highest point.

父在、父没统贯以观。

【英译文】

The Master (Confucius) said, While a man's father is alive, you can only observe his intentions; when his father dies, you observe his action. If for the whole three years of mourning he manages to carry on the household exactly as in his father's day, then he is a good son indeed.

1.12

有子曰：“礼之用[1]，和为贵。先王之道[2]，斯为美。小大由之。有所不行，知和而和，不以礼节之[3]，亦不可行也。”

【中译文】

有子说：“礼的应用，以处理事情自然和谐为可贵。古代贤王的治道也以此为美。小事大事，都按照这个原则。也有不按此行事的时候，即为和谐而和谐，不用礼来调节和约束，那也是不可以的。”

【注释】

1 礼：指周礼。周代先王留下的仪礼制度。
2 王：指周文王等古代的贤王。
3 节：节制，约束。

【英译文】

You Zi said, In carrying out the rites, it is harmony that is prized ; the way of the former kings from this got its beauty. Both small matters and great depend upon it. If things go amiss, he who knows the harmony will be able to attune them. But if harmony itself is not modulated by ritual, things will still go amiss.

1.13

有子曰：“信近于义[1]，言可复也[2]。恭近于礼，远耻辱也[3]。因不失其亲[4]，亦可宗也[5]。”

【中译文】

有子说：“讲信用，要于义相符，其信约承诺才能得到实践与兑现。恭敬，要于礼相符，才能避免耻辱。所依靠的，应当是可以亲近的人，只有这样的人在关键时候能有所担当。”

【注释】

1 近：符合，接近。义：合理的，有道理的，符合于周礼的。
2 复：实践，实行。
3 远：避免，免去。
4 因：依靠，凭借。
5 宗：尊奉，尊崇，可靠。

论语意解

1.15

子贡曰："贫而无谄，富而无骄，何如？"子曰"可也，未若贫而乐，富而好礼者也。"子贡曰："《诗》云：'如切如磋，如琢如磨。'[1] 其斯之谓与？"子曰："赐也，始可与言《诗》已矣，告诸往而知来者[2]。"

【中译文】

子贡说："贫穷而不谄媚，富裕而不骄横，怎么样呢？"孔子说："也算可以了，但是，还不如贫穷不失快乐，富裕而爱好礼义。"子贡说："《诗经》说：'像切磋兽骨象牙，像琢磨美石宝玉。'就是讲的这个意思吧？"孔子说："端木赐呀，我可以开始同你谈论《诗经》了。告诉你已经发生的事，你已经可以据此预知未来的事了。"

【注 释】

1 "如切"句：出自《诗经·卫风·淇奥》篇。"切"，古代把骨头加工成器物，叫切。"磋（cuō）"，把象牙加工成器物。"琢（zhuó）"，雕刻玉石，做成器物。"磨"，把石头加工成器物。
2 "告诸"句："诸"，"之于"的合音。"往"，已发生的事，已知的事。"来"，尚未发生的事，未知的事。

论语意解

一四

【英译文】

You Zi said, If your promises cleaves to what is right, you will be able to fulfil your word. If your obeisances cleaves to ritual, you will keep dishonour at bay. Marry one who has not betrayed her own kin, And you may safely present her to your Ancestors.

1.14

子曰："君子食无求饱，居无求安，敏于事而慎于言，就有道而正焉[1]，可谓好学也已。"

【中译文】

孔子说："君子吃饭不追求饱足，居住不追求舒适，做事果决，说话谨慎，向有道德的人看齐，并使之作为榜样时时匡正自己，这样做就可以称得上好学了。"

【注 释】

1 就：靠近，接近。

【英译文】

The Master (Confucius) said, A gentleman who never goes on eating till he is sated, who does not demand comfort at home, who is diligent in business and cautious in speech, who associates with those that possess the Way and thereby corrects his own faults-such a one may indeed be said to have a taste for learning.

一三

1.15

子贡曰:"贫而无谄,富而无骄,何如?"子曰:"可也,未若贫而乐,富而好礼者也。"子贡曰:"《诗》云:'如切如磋,如琢如磨。'其斯之谓与?"子曰:"赐也,始可与言《诗》已矣,告诸往而知来者。"

【中译文】

子贡说:"贫穷而不谄媚,富裕而不骄傲,怎么样呢?""不错呀,"此其可以了,"他说,"还不如贫穷而乐、富裕而爱好礼义。"子贡说:"《诗经》说:'像象牙经过切磋,像美玉经过琢磨。'就是讲的这个意思吧?""孔子说:"赐呀,我可以开始同你谈论《诗经》了。告诉你已经发生的事,你已经可以推知和未来的事了。"

【注释】

1."如切如磋"句:出自《诗经·卫风·淇奥》篇。"切",古代把兽骨加工成器物,叫切。"磋(cuō)",把象牙加工成器物。"琢(zhuó)",雕刻玉石,做成器物。"磨",把石头加工成器物。

2."告诸"句:"诸","之于"的合音。"往",已发生的事,已知的事。"来",尚未发生的事,未知的事。

【英译文】

You Zi said, If your promises cleaves to what is right, you will be able to fulfil your word. If your obeisances cleaves to ritual, you will keep dishonour at bay. Many one who has not betrayed her own kin. And you may safely present her to your Ancestors.

1.14

子曰:"君子食无求饱,居无求安,敏于事而慎于言,就有道而正焉,可谓好学也已。"

【中译文】

孔子说:"君子吃饭不追求饱足,居住不追求安逸,做事勤快敏捷,向有道德的人看齐,这样做就可以称得上好学了。"

【注释】

1.就:靠近,接近。

【英译文】

The Master (Confucius) said, A gentleman who never goes on eating till he is sated, who does not demand comfort at home, who is diligent in business and cautious in speech, who associates with those that possess the Way and thereby corrects his own faults-such a one may indeed be said to have a taste for learning.

【英译文】

Zi Gong said, 'Poor without cadging, rich without swagger.' What of that? The Master said, Not bad. But better still, 'Poor, yet delighting in the Way, rich, yet a student of ritual.' Zi Gong said, The saying of the songs, as thing cut, as thing filed, as thing chiselled, as thing polished refers, I suppose, to what you have just said? The Master said, Ssu, now I can really begin to talk to you about the Songs, for When I have told you what precedes, you know what follows.

1.16

子曰:"不患人之不己知[1],患不知人也。"

【中译文】

孔子说:"不要担心别人不了解自己,怕的是自己不了解别人。"

【注释】

1 不己知:"不知己"的倒装句。"知",了解,理解。此句可与"人不知而不愠,不亦君子乎"参酌看。

【英译文】

The Master (Confucius) said, The good man is not worried that other people do not recognize his merits. His only anxiety is lest he should fail to recognize theirs.

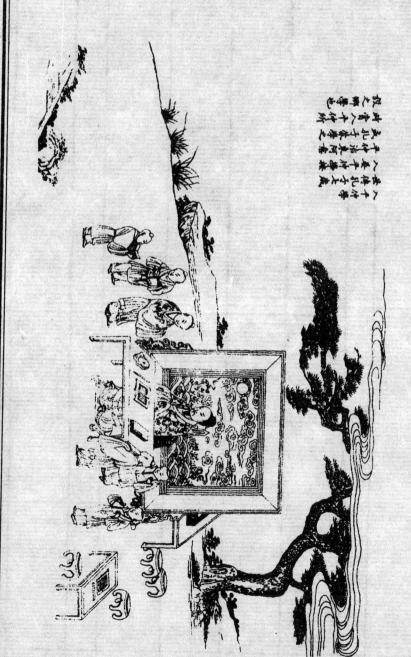

入平仲学 Learning at the school Sponsored by Yan Pingzhong

论语意解

【英译文】

Zi Gong said, 'Poor without cadging, rich without swagger. What of that?' The Master said, 'Not bad. But better still, "Poor, yet delighting in the Way, rich, yet a student of ritual." Zi Gong said, 'The saying of the songs, as thing cut, as thing filed, as thing chiselled, as thing polished refers, I suppose, to what you have just said?' The Master said, 'Ssu, now I can really begin to talk to you about the Songs, for, When I have told you what precedes, you know what follows.'

1·16

子曰："不患人之不己知，患不知人也。"

【中译文】

孔子说："不要愁别人不了解自己，愁的是自己不了解别人。"

【注释】

1 不己知："不知己"的倒装句。"知"，了解。理解，此句可与"人不知而不愠，不亦君子乎"参阅看。

【英译文】

The Master (Confucius) said, 'The good man is not worried that other people do not recognize his merits. His only anxiety is lest he should fail to recognize theirs.'

可以说是：'思想纯朴，没有刻意虚假的东西。'"

【注释】

1 蔽（bì）：概括，包盖。

2 思无邪：原出《诗经·鲁颂·駉》篇。孔子借用这句话来评论《诗经》。朱熹《四书章句集注》：程子曰：思无邪者，诚也。

【英译文】

The Master (Confucius) said, If out of the three hundred Songs I had to take one phrase to cover all my teaching, I should say 'Let there be no evil in your thoughts.'

2.3

子曰："道之以政[1]，齐之以刑[2]，民免而无耻[3]；道之以德，齐之以礼，有耻且格[4]。"

【中译文】

孔子说："用政策来管理、用刑法来整治，人们会避免犯罪，但心里不认为犯罪是可耻的；用道德教化来管理，用礼制来规范，人们就会有羞耻之心，而且会自觉匡正自身的行为。"

【注释】

1 道：同"导"。管理，引导。

2 齐：整治，约束，统一。

论语意解

一一
八七

为政篇第二（共二十四章）

On Governing

2.1

子曰："为政以德，譬如北辰[1]，居其所而众星共之[2]。"

【中译文】

孔子说："用道德教化来治理国家，就好像北极星一样，处于它自己的方位上，群星都环绕着它。"

【注释】

1 北辰：北极星。

2 共：同"拱"。环绕。

【英译文】

The Master (Confucius) said, He who rules by moral force is like the pole-star, which remains in its place while all the other stars surround it.

2.2

子曰："《诗》三百，一言以蔽之[1]，曰：'思无邪[2]。'"

【中译文】

孔子说："《诗经》三百篇，用一句话来概括它，

为政篇第二 （共二十四章）

On Governing

2.1

子曰："为政以德，譬如北辰，居其所而众星共之。"

【中译文】

孔子说："用道德教化来治理国家，就好像北极星一样，安于自己的方位上，群星都环绕着它。"

【注释】

1 北辰：北极星。

2 共：同"拱"，环绕，环抱。

【英译文】

The Master (Confucius) said, He who rules by moral force is like the pole-star, which remains in its place while all the other stars surround it.

2.2

子曰："《诗》三百，一言以蔽之，曰：'思无邪。'"

【中译文】

孔子说："《诗经》三百篇，用一句话来概括它，

【注释】

1 蔽（bì）：概括，囊括。

2 思无邪：语出《诗经·鲁颂·駉》篇，"孔子借用这句来评价整部《诗经》。未尝《四书章句集注》：程子曰：思无邪者，诚也。"

【英译文】

The Master (Confucius) said, If out of the three hundred Songs I had to take one phrase to cover all my teaching, I should say If there be no evil in your thoughts.

2.3

子曰："道之以政，齐之以刑，民免而无耻；道之以德，齐之以礼，有耻且格。"

【中译文】

孔子说："用政法来诱导，用刑罚来整治，人们只求免于犯罪受惩罚，却没有羞耻心；用道德来诱导，用礼教来规范，人们就会有廉耻之心，而且会自觉走上正路。"

【注释】

1 道：同"导"，诱导，引导。

2 齐：整治，约束，规范。

赋与天性、人生的道义和职责等多重含义。

【英译文】

The Master (Confucius) said, At fifteen I set my heart upon learning. At thirty, I was firmly established. At forty, I had no more doubts. At fifty, I knew what were the biddings of Heaven. At sixty, I heard them with docile ear. At seventy, I could follow the dictates of my own heart; for what I desired no longer overstepped the boundaries of right.

2.5

　　孟懿子问孝[1]，子曰："无违。"樊迟御[2]，子告之曰："孟孙问孝于我，我对曰：'无违。'"樊迟曰："何谓也？"子曰："生，事之以礼；死，葬之以礼，祭之以礼。"

【中译文】

　　孟懿子请教孔子怎样做是孝，孔子说："不违背。"樊迟为孔子赶马车，孔子对他说："孟孙氏问我怎样做是孝，我回答他：'不违背。'"樊迟说："是什么意思呢？"孔子说："父母在世时，按礼制侍奉他们；去世了，要按礼制为他们办丧事，按礼制祭祀他们。"

【注释】

1 孟懿（yì）子：姓仲孙，亦即孟孙，名何忌，"懿"是谥号。鲁国大夫。与叔孙氏、季孙氏共同把执鲁

3 免：避免，指避免犯错误。无耻：做了坏事，心里不知羞耻；没有羞耻之心。

4 格：正，纠正。

【英译文】

The Master (Confucius) said, Govern the people by regulations, keep order among them by punishment, and they will flee from you, and lose all self-respect. Govern them by moral force, keep order among them by ritual and they will keep their self-respect and come to you of their own accord.

2.4

　　子曰："吾十有五而志于学[1]，三十而立，四十而不惑，五十而知天命[2]，六十而耳顺，七十而从心所欲，不逾矩。"

【中译文】

　　孔子说："我十五岁时开始立志于学问；三十岁时能自立于世；四十岁时不再迷惑；五十岁时懂得了自己的天命；六十岁时能听得进不同的意见；七十岁时想做什么就做什么，却处处符合礼制。"

【注释】

1 有：同"又"。表示相加。"十有五"，即十加五，十五岁。

2 天命：这里的"天命"含有上天的意旨、自然的禀

做与天性、人生的道义和取胜等意义相符。

【英译文】

The Master (Confucius) said, At fifteen I set my heart upon learning. At thirty I was firmly established. At forty, I had no more doubts. At fifty, I knew what were the biddings of Heaven. At sixty, I heard them with docile ear. At seventy, I could follow the dictates of my own heart; for what I desired no longer overstepped the boundaries of right.

2.5

孟懿子问孝。子曰:"无违。"樊迟御,子告之曰:"孟孙问孝于我,我对曰:'无违。'"樊迟曰:"何谓也?"子曰:"生,事之以礼;死,葬之以礼,祭之以礼。"

【中译文】

孟懿子向孔子请教怎样是孝道。孔子说:"不违背。"后来孟懿子的儿子孟武伯,为孔子驾车赶路,孔子对他说:"孟孙向我问孝,我回答说:'不违背。'"樊迟说:"是什么意思呢?"孔子说:"父母在世时,按礼制侍奉他们;去世了,要按礼制为他们办丧事,按礼制祭祀他们。"

【注释】

1 孟懿(yì)子:鲁国大夫仲孙何忌,谥号懿。"懿"考温柔圣善。子,对男子的尊称。曾向孔子学礼。

【英译文】

The Master (Confucius) said, Govern the people by regulations, keep order among them by punishment, and they will flee from you, and lose all self respect. Govern them by moral force, keep order among them by ritual and they will keep their self-respect and come to you of their own accord.

2.4

子曰:"吾十有五而志于学,三十而立,四十而不惑,五十而知天命,六十而耳顺,七十而从心所欲,不逾矩。"

【中译文】

孔子说:"我十五岁时立志致力于学问;三十岁能自立于世;四十岁遇事不再迷惑;五十岁便懂得了自己的天命;六十岁时能听得进各种不同的意见;七十岁时想做什么就做什么,却总也不越出规矩。"

【注释】

1 有:同"又"。常用于整数加零数,"十有五",即十五。

2 天命:含有上天的意旨,自然的禀赋

【英译文】

Meng Wubo asked about the treatment of parents. The Master said, Behave in such a way that your father and mother have no anxiety about you, except concerning your health.

2.7

子游问孝[1]，子曰："今之孝者，是谓能养。至于犬马，皆能有养。不敬，何以别乎？"

【中译文】

子游问怎样做是孝，孔子说："现在所谓孝顺，总说能够供养父母就可以了。可是人也都能做到饲养狗与马。如果对父母不诚心孝敬的话，那和饲养狗马有什么区别呢？"

【注释】

1 子游：姓言，名偃（yǎn），字子游。吴国人。生于公元前506年，卒年不详。孔子的弟子。比孔子小四十五岁。

【英译文】

Zi You asked about the treatment of parents. The Master said, 'Filial sons' nowadays are people who see to it that their parents get enough to eat. But even dogs and horses are cared for to that extent. If they don't show respect for their parents, where lies the difference between parents and

---

国朝政。

2 樊（fán）迟：姓樊，名须，字子迟。孔子的弟子。曾与冉（rǎn）求一起为季康子做事。生于公元前515年，卒年不详，比孔子小四十六岁。御：赶车，驾车。

【英译文】

Meng yi zi asked about the treatment of parents. The master said, never disobey! When fan chi was driving his carriage for him, the master said, meng asked me about the treatment of parents and I said, never disobey! Fan chi said, in what sense did you mean it? The master said, While they are alive, serve them according to ritual. When they die, bury them according to ritual and sacrifice to them according to ritual.

2.6

孟武伯问孝[1]。子曰："父母，唯其疾之忧[2]。"

【中译文】

孟武伯问怎样做是孝。孔子说："做父母的只须担忧子女的疾病。"（不必为其他方面担忧，所以子女之自立，能免父母之忧，也是孝敬的表现。）

【注释】

1 孟武伯：姓仲孙，名彘（zhì），孟懿子的儿子。"武"是谥号。

2 其：代词，指子女，"疾"指疾病。

论语意解

论语意解

2.6

孟武伯问孝。子曰："父母唯其疾之忧。"

【中译文】

孟武伯问怎样是孝，孔子说："（对父母，）做儿女的只是为他们的疾病发愁。（不必为其他事担忧。）"

【注释】

1. 孟武伯：即仲孙，名彘（zhì），是懿子仲孙何忌的儿子。"武"是谥号。

2. 其：代词，指父母。疾：病。唯其疾：指疾病。

【英译文】

Meng Yi zi asked about the treatment of parents. The master said, never disobey! When Fan chi was driving his carriage for him, the master said, meng asked me about the treatment of parents and I said, never disobey! Fan chi said, in what sense did you mean it? The master said, While they are alive, serve them according to ritual. When they die, bury them according to ritual and sacrifice to them according to ritual.

2.7

子游问孝。子曰："今之孝者，是谓能养。至于犬马，皆能有养。不敬，何以别乎？"

【中译文】

子游问怎样是孝，孔子说："现在所谓孝顺，指的是能够养活爹娘便行了。可是，对狗马也都能饲养；若不存心严肃地孝顺父母，那养活爹娘和饲养狗马又有什么去区别呢？"

【注释】

1. 子游：姓言，名偃（yǎn），字子游，吴国人，生于公元前506年，少孔子四十五岁，孔子的弟子，比孔子小四十五岁。

【英译文】

Zi You asked about the treatment of parents. The Master said, "Filial sons nowadays are people who see to it that their parents get enough to eat. But even dogs and horses are cared for to that extent. If they don't show respect for their parents, where lies the difference between parents and..."

【英译文】

Meng Wubo asked about the treatment of parents. The Master said, "Behave in such a way that your father and mother have no anxiety about you except concerning your health."

---

2. 孟（mèng）：孟孙。名彘，字子烝，孟懿子的儿子，曾从孔子学习。懿子死后，孟武伯继位，生于公元前515年，少孔子三十四岁。"武"是谥号，"伯"是排行。

2.9

子曰："吾与回言终日[1]，不违，如愚。退而省其私[2]，亦足以发，回也不愚。"

【中译文】

孔子说："我和颜回讲话一整天，他毫无不同的意见，似乎很愚笨。然而考察他私下里的言行，却发现他对我所讲的话能够很好发挥并实践，颜回并不是愚笨的。"

【注释】

1 回：姓颜，名回。字子渊，又称颜渊。鲁国人。生于公元前521年（一说，公元前511年），卒于公元前480年。是孔子早年最忠实的弟子，被孔子器重、厚爱。比孔子小三十（一说四十）岁。

2 省（xǐng）：观察，考察。

【英译文】

The Master (Confucius) said, I can talk to Yan Hui a whole day without his ever differing from me. One would think he was stupid. But if I enquire into his private conduct when he is not with me I find that it fully demonstrates what I have taught him. No, Hui is by no means stupid.

2.10

子曰："视其所以[1]，观其所由[2]，察其所安。

---

animals?

2.8

子夏问孝，子曰："色难[1]。有事，弟子服其劳[2]；有酒食，先生馔[3]，曾是以为孝乎[4]？"

【中译文】

子夏问怎样做是孝，孔子说："对父母一直和颜悦色是难的。有了事，孩子为父母去做；有了酒饭，让父母吃，但仅仅这样就能算是孝吗？"

【注释】

1 色：脸色。指和颜悦色；心里敬爱父母，脸面上好看。

2 弟子：晚辈。指儿女。

3 先生：长辈。指父母。馔（zhuàn）：吃喝。

4 曾（zēng）：副词。难道。是：代词。此，这个。

【英译文】

Zi Xia asked about the treatment of parents. The Master said, It is difficult for a son to have a pleasant facial expression all the time. Filial piety does not consist merely in young people undertaking the hard work, when anything has to be done, or serving their elders first with wine and food. It is something much more than that.

論語淺釋

2.9

子曰："吾见回言终日，不违，如愚。退而
省其私，亦足以发，回也不愚。"

【中译文】

孔子说："我和颜回谈论话语一整天，他总是不同的意
见，好像很愚笨。但而是考察他私下里的言行，却发现
他对我所讲的话能够很好地发挥实践，颜回并不是愚
笨的。"

【注释】

1. 回：颜回，名回，字子渊，又称颜渊，鲁国人。
生于公元前521年（一说，公元前511年），卒于公
元前480年。是孔子早年最忠实的弟子，被孔子器
重、喜爱。出《孔子十子十一（一说四十）岁。

2. 省（xíng）：观察，考察。

【英译文】

The Master (Confucius) said, I can talk to Yan Hui a whole day without
his ever differing from me. One would think he was stupid. But If I enquire into
his private conduct when he is not with me I find that it fully demonstrates
what I have taught him. No, Hui is by no means stupid.

2.10

子曰："视其所以，观其所由，察其所安。

2.8

子夏问孝。子曰："色难。有事，弟子服其
劳；有酒食，先生馔，曾是以为孝乎？"

【中译文】

子夏问怎样做是孝。孔子说："对父母一直和颜悦
色是难的。有了事，弟子为父母去做；有了酒饭，让
父母吃，他们以为这样就算是孝了吗？"

【注释】

1. 色：脸色。指和颜悦色；特别是侍奉父母，脸面上
的神态。

2. 弟子：晚辈。指儿女。

3. 先生：长辈。指父母。馔（zhuàn）：吃喝。

4. 曾（zēng）：副词，难道，岂。竟，竟然。此，这个。

【英译文】

Zi Xia asked about the treatment of parents. The Master said, It is difficult
for a son to have a pleasant facial expression all the time. Filial piety does not
consist merely in young people undertaking the hard work, when anything has
to be done, or serving their elders first with wine and food. It is something
much more than that.

样的人可以做老师了。

【注释】

1 故：旧的，原先的。

【英译文】

The Master (Confucius) said, He who by reviewing the old can gain knowledge of the New is fit to be a teacher.

2.12

子曰："君子不器[1]。"

【中译文】

孔子说："君子不要像器具。"

【注释】

1 器：器具。只有一种固定用途的东西。比喻人只具备一种知识，一种才能，一种技艺。强调君子不拘于一能一技，而应当有所超越、因地制宜、因势利导。

【英译文】

The Master (Confucius) said, A gentleman is not an implement, which only has one specific use.

论语意解

人焉廋哉[3]？人焉廋哉？"

【中译文】

从他的行为上看，从他的动机上分析，再考察他安心于做什么。这样，人怎么能隐瞒得了呢？人怎么能隐瞒得了呢？"

【注释】

1 以：根据，原因，言行的动机。一说，"以"，通"与"。引申为与谁。同谁，结交什么样的朋友。
2 由：经由，走的道路。指为达到目的而采用的方式方法。
3 焉：代词，表疑问。哪里，怎么。廋（sōu）：隐藏，隐瞒。

【英译文】

The Master (Confucius) said, Look closely into his aims, observe the means by which he pursues them, discover what brings him content. And then can the man's real character remain hidden from you, can it remain hidden from you?

2.11

子曰："温故而知新[1]，可以为师矣。"

【中译文】

从过去的经历与知识中能不断挖掘出新的东西，这样的人才不能去侮辱了。

【注释】

1. 故:旧的。温:复习的。

【英译文】

The Master (Confucius) said, He who by reviewing the old can gain knowledge of the New is fit to be a teacher.

2.12

子曰:"君子不器。"

【中译文】

孔子说:"君子不是像器具。"

【注释】

1. 器:器具。只有一种固定用途的东西。比喻人只具备一种知识,一种技艺。懂得礼义,通晓事理,因地制宜,因物制宜。

【英译文】

The Master (Confucius) said, A gentleman is not an implement, which only has one specific use.

人焉廋哉?人焉廋哉?"

【中译文】

从他的行为来看,从他的动机上分析,再考察他安心于什么。这样,人怎么么能信得隐瞒得了呢?人怎么么能信得隐瞒得了呢?

【注释】

1. 以:根据。所以,所因,言行的动机。一,同"以",通"与"。引申为安,同物。看文选取目的而来用的方式。

2. 由:经由。无指途径。

3. 焉:代词。表疑问。哪里。廋:sou;隐藏。隐瞒。

【英译文】

The Master (Confucius) said, Look closely into his aims, observe the means by which he pursues them, discover what brings him content. And then can the man's real character remain hidden from you?

2.11

子曰:"温故而知新,可以为师矣。"

【中译文】

从过去的经历所得知的东西中都不断发掘出新的东西,就

【英译文】

The Master (Confucius) said, A gentleman can see a question from all sides without bias. The petty man does the reverse.

2.15

子曰："学而不思则罔[1]，思而不学则殆[2]。"

【中译文】

孔子说："学习而不思考，就会迷惑；思考而不学习，则会偏离正道。"

【注释】

1 思：思考，思维。罔（wǎng）：同惘。迷惑，昏而无得。

2 殆（dài）：危险，偏离正道。

【英译文】

The Master (Confucius) said, 'He who learns but does not think, is lost.' He who thinks but does not learn is in great danger.

2.16

子曰："攻乎异端[1]，斯害也已[2]。"

【中译文】

孔子说："去攻读钻研异端邪说，那很有害呀。"

2.13

子贡问君子，子曰："先行其言而后从之。"

【中译文】

子贡问怎样做才是君子，孔子说："在说之前，先去实行，然后再说出来。"

【英译文】

Zi Gong asked about the true gentleman. The Master said, He does not preach what he prastices till he has practised what he preaches.

2.14

子曰："君子周而不比[1]。小人比而不周[2]。"

【中译文】

孔子说："君子能团结众人，但不结党营私；小人善于结党营私而不团结众人。"

【注释】

1 周：同周围的人相处得很好，合群，团结。比（bì）：本义是并列，挨着。在这里有贬义：为私情而勾结，拉帮结伙，结党营私。

2 小人：不正派、不道德、人格卑鄙的人。古代也称地位低的人。

论语意解

2.13

子贡问君子。子曰："先行其言而后从之。"

【中译文】

子贡问怎样才是君子，孔子说："对于你要说的话，先实行了，然后再说出来。"

【英译文】

Zi Gong asked about the true gentleman. The Master said, He does not preach what he has practised till he preaches.

2.14

子曰："君子周而不比，小人比而不周。"

【中译文】

孔子说："君子团结众人而不互相勾结，小人互相勾结而不团结众人。"

【注释】

1. 周：同周围的人相处得很好。合群，团结。比(bǐ)：本义是并列。勾结。在这里有贬义：勾结营私。而和比结合，指相结私、搞宗派私。

2. 小人：不正派、不道德，人格卑鄙龌龊的人。古代也指地位低的人。

【英译文】

The Master (Confucius) said, A gentleman can see a question from all sides without bias. The petty man does the reverse.

2.15

子曰："学而不思则罔，思而不学则殆。"

【中译文】

孔子说："学习而不思考，就会迷惑；思考而不学习，那就危险了。"

【注释】

1. 思：思考，思维。罔(wǎng)：同惘。迷惑，昏而无所得。

2. 殆(dài)：疑惑，精神疲怠。

【英译文】

The Master (Confucius) said, 'He who learns but does not think, is lost. He who thinks but does not learn is in great danger.

2.16

子曰："攻乎异端，斯害也已。"

【中译文】

孔子说："专攻奇谈怪论邪说，那是很有害的。"

【注释】

1 攻：指学习攻读，专治，钻研。一说，攻击。异端：不同的学说、主张。

2 斯：代词。这，那。已：语气词，表慨叹，相当"矣"。

【英译文】

The Master (Confucius) said, He who sets to work upon a different strand destroys the whole fabric.

2.17

子曰："由[1]，诲女[2]知之乎？知之为知之，不知为不知，是知也[3]。"

【中译文】

孔子说："仲由，我告诉你怎样学到知识吧。知道就是知道，不知道就是不知道，这才是真正的'知道'。"

【注释】

1 由：姓仲，名由，字子路，又字季路。鲁国卞（今山东省平邑县东北）人。是孔子早年的弟子。长期跟随孔子，是忠实的警卫。曾做季康子的家臣，后死于卫国内乱。生于公元前524年，卒于公元前480年，比孔子小九岁。

2 诲（huì）：教导，教育，诱导。女：同"汝"。你。

---

3 知：前五个"知"字，是知道，了解，懂得。最后"是知也"的"知"，同"智"。明智，聪明，真知。之：代词。指孔子所讲授的知识、学问。

【英译文】

The Master (Confucius) said, Zhong You shall I teach you what knowledge is? When you know a thing, say that you know it, and when you do not know a thing, admit that you do not know it. That is knowledge.

2.18

子张学干禄[1]。子曰："多闻阙疑[2]，慎言其馀，其寡尤[3]；多见阙殆，慎行其馀，则寡悔。言寡尤，行寡悔，禄在其中矣。"

【中译文】

子张学习如何求官进阶。孔子说："要多听，把觉得可怀疑的地方避开，谨慎地说出有把握的，这样就能少犯错误；要多看，把觉得有危险的事情避开，谨慎地去做有把握的，这样就能减少后悔。说话少出错，做事少后悔，谋求官职的秘诀就在其中了。"

【注释】

1 子张：姓颛（zhuān）孙，名师，字子张。陈国人。孔子晚年的弟子，比孔子小四十八岁。生于公元前503年，卒年不详。干禄：求仕，谋求做官。"干"，

论语意解

【注释】

3 知：前五个"知"字，基础意思是了解，懂得。最后一个"是知也"的"知"，同"智"，明智，聪明。其实，之：代词，指孔子所讲授的知识，学问。

【英译文】

The Master (Confucius) said, Zhong You, shall I teach you what knowledge is? When you know a thing, say that you know it, and when you do not know a thing, admit that you do not know it. That is knowledge.

2.18

子张学干禄。子曰："多闻阙疑，慎言其余，则寡尤；多见阙殆，慎行其余，则寡悔。言寡尤，行寡悔，禄在其中矣。"

【中译文】

子张学习如何来谋取官职。孔子说："要多听，有怀疑的地方先放在一旁不说，谨慎地说出那些足有把握的，这样就能减少错误；要多看，有怀疑的地方先放在一旁不做，谨慎地去做那些有把握的，这样就能减少懊悔。说话少错误，做事少懊悔，谋求官职的诀窍就在其中了。"

【注释】

1 子张：姓颛孙（zhuān），名师，字子张，陈国人。孔子晚年的弟子，比孔子小四十八岁，生于公元前503年。学干禄：干禄，求禄。干，求；禄，官吏的俸禄。

【注释】

1 攻：指专习攻治。异端：不同的学说，主张。
2 斯：代词，这，此。也已：句末语气词，表肯定，相当于"矣"。

【英译文】

The Master (Confucius) said, He who sets to work upon a different strand destroys the whole fabric.

2.17

子曰："由，诲女知之乎！知之为知之，不知为不知，是知也。"

【中译文】

孔子说："仲由，来告诉你怎样才能算知道吧：知道就是知道，不知道就是不知道，这才是真正的知道。"

【注释】

1 由：姓仲，名由，字子路，又字季路，春秋末年鲁国卞（今山东省平邑县东北）人。是孔子早年的弟子，长期追随孔子，是忠实的警卫，曾做季氏的宰臣。生于公元前521年，率于公元前480年，仅比孔子小九岁。
2 诲（huì）：教导，教诲。女：同"汝"，你。

求，谋。"禄"，官吏的俸禄，官职。

2 阙(què)：空，缺，有所保留。

3 寡：少。尤：过错，错误。

【英译文】

Zi Zhang asked the Master how to obtain an official preferment. The Master said, Hear much, but maintain silence as regards doubtful points and be cautious in speaking of the rest; then you will seldom get into trouble. See much, but ignore what it is dangerous to have seen, and be cautious in acting upon the rest; then you will seldom want to undo your acts. He who seldom gets into trouble about what he has said and seldom does anything that he afterwards wishes he had not done, will be sure incidentally to get his reward.

2.19

哀公问曰[1]："何为则民服[2]？"孔子对曰："举直错诸枉[3]，则民服；举枉错诸直，则民不服。"

【中译文】

鲁哀公问："怎样做才能让老百姓信服呢？"孔子回答说："选拔正直的人，废弃邪恶的人，老百姓就信服；选拔邪恶的人，废弃正直的人，老百姓就不信服了。"

【注释】

1 哀公：鲁国鲁定公的儿子，姓姬，名蒋。"哀"是死后的谥号。在位二十七年(自公元前494年至公元前466年)。

2 何为：怎样做，做什么。

3 举：选拔，推举。直：正直的、正派的人。错：废置，舍弃。一说，错同"措"，安排。诸："之于"的合音。枉：不正直、不正派、邪恶的人。

【英译文】

Duke Ai asked, What shall I do so that I can get the support of the common people? Master replied, If you 'raise up the straight and set them on top of the crooked,' the commoners will support you. But if you raise the crooked and set them on top of the straight, the commoners will not support you.

2.20

季康子问[1]："使民敬，忠以劝[2]，如之何？"子曰："临之以庄[3]，则敬；孝慈，则忠；举善而教不能，则劝。"

【中译文】

季康子问："要博得老百姓的敬意，忠诚并相互支持勉励，应该如何做呢？"孔子说："你要用庄重严肃的态度来对待他们，就会博得尊重；你倡导对父母孝顺，对众人慈爱，他们就会忠实于你；你选拔任用善良优秀的人，又教育那些能力差的人，人民就会互相

论语意解

【注释】

米、禄:"禄",官吏的俸禄、官职。

2 阙(què):空,缺,有所保留。

3 寡:少。尤:过错,错误。悔:悔恨。

【英译文】

Zi Zhang asked the Master how to obtain an official preferment. The Master said, Hear much, but maintain silence as regards doubtful points and be cautious in speaking of the rest; then you will seldom get into trouble. See much, but ignore what it is dangerous to have seen, and be cautious in acting upon the rest; then you will seldom want to undo your acts. He who seldom gets into trouble about what he has said and seldom does anything that he afterwards wishes he had not done, will be sure incidentally to get his reward.

2.19

哀公问曰:"何为则民服?"孔子对曰:"举直错诸枉,则民服;举枉错诸直,则民不服。"

【中译文】

鲁哀公问:"怎样做才能让老百姓信服呢?"孔子回答说:"选拔正直的人,废弃邪恶的人,老百姓就会信服;选拔邪恶的人,废弃正直的人,老百姓就不信服了。"

【注释】

1 哀公:鲁国君主定公的儿子,鲁定公的儿子,名蒋,"哀"是

死后的谥号。在位二十七年(自公元前494年至公元前466年)。

2 何为:怎样做,做什么。

3 举:选拔,提拔。直:正直的,正派的人。错:废置,舍弃。一说,错同"措",安排。诸:"之于"的合音。枉:不正直,不正派,邪恶的人。

【英译文】

Duke Ai asked, What shall I do so that I can get the support of the common people? Master replied, If you 'raise up the straight and set them on top of the crooked, the commoners will support you. But if you raise the crooked and set them on top of the straight, the commoners will not support you.

2.20

季康子问:"使民敬、忠以劝,如之何?"子曰:"临之以庄,则敬;孝慈,则忠;举善而教不能,则劝。"

【中译文】

季康子问:"要使得老百姓严肃认真、尽心竭力和互相勉励,应该如何做呢?"孔子说:"你对待百姓庄重认真,他们就会严肃认真;你讲究孝慈,人民就会尽心竭力;你选拔善良的人,又教育能力差的人,人民就会互相勉励。"

倡导孝悌的道理可以影响到政治。' 这就是从政，为什么非得做官才算是从政呢？"

【注释】

1 或：代词。有人。

2 奚：疑问词。何，怎么。

3 书：指《尚书》。是商周时期的政治文告和历史资料的汇编，孔子在这里引用的三句，见于伪古文《尚书·君陈》篇。

4 施：推广，延及，影响于。有：助词，无意义。

5 "奚其"句："奚"，为什么。"其"，代词，指做官。"为"，是。"为政"，参与政治。鲁定公初年，孔子没有出来做官，所以，有人疑其不为政。

【英译文】

Someone said to Confucius, How is it that you are not in the public service? The Master said, The Book of history says: 'Be filial, only be filial and friendly towards your brothers, and you will be contributing to government.' There are other sorts of service quite different from what you mean by service.

2.22

子曰："人而无信[1]，不知其可也。大车无輗[2]，小车无軏[3]，其何以行之哉[4]？"

论语意解

勉励而努力干了。"

【注释】

1 季康子：姓季孙，名肥。"康"是谥号。"子"，是尊称。鲁哀公时，任正卿（宰相），政治上最有势力。

2 以：连词。而。劝：勉励。

3 临：对待。

【英译文】

Ji Kangzi asked how to get the common people to be respectful and loyal and encourage each other. The Master said, Approach them with dignity, and they will respect you. Show piety towards your parents and kindness towards your children, and they will be loyal to you, Promote those who are worthy, train those who are incompetent; that is the best form of encouragement.

2.21

或谓孔子曰[1]："子奚不为政[2]？"子曰："《书》云[3]：'孝乎惟孝，友于兄弟，施于有政[4]。'是亦为政，奚其为为政[5]？"

【中译文】

有人对孔子说："你为什么不从政呢？"孔子说："《尚书》里有句话说：'孝啊就是孝敬父母，友爱兄弟。

【注释】

1　季康子：姓季孙，名肥。"康"，是谥号。"子"，是尊称。曾执公职，任正卿（宰相），政治上最有权力。

2　以：连词，而。劝：勉励。

3　临：对待。

【英译文】

Ji Kangzi asked how to get the common people to be respectful and loyal and encourage each other. The Master said, Approach them with dignity, and they will respect you. Show piety towards your parents and kindness towards your children, and they will be loyal to you. Promote those who are worthy, train those who are incompetent; that is the best form of encouragement.

2.21

或谓孔子曰："子奚不为政²？"子曰："《书》³云：'孝乎惟孝，友于兄弟，施于有政⁴。'是亦为政，奚其为为政⁵？"

【中译文】

有人对孔子说："您为什么不从政呢？"孔子说："《尚书》里有句话说：'孝啊就是孝敬父母，友爱兄弟，

倡导孝悌的道理可以影响到政治，这就是从政。为什么非得做官才算是从政呢？"

【注释】

1　或：代词，有人。

2　奚：疑问词，何，怎么。

3　书：指《尚书》，是商周时期的政治公文和史资料的汇编。孔子在这里所引用的三句，见于伪古文《尚书·君陈》篇。

4　施：推广。迤及，扩散到。有：如同，无意义。

5　奚其为：句。"奚"，"其"，代词，指疑问。"为"，是，"为政"，参与政治，鲁定公初年，孔子没有出来做官，所以，有人疑其不为政。

【英译文】

Someone said to Confucius, How is it that you are not in the public service? The Master said, The Book of history says; Be filial, only be filial and friendly towards your brothers, and you will be contributing to government. There are other sorts of service quite different from what you mean by service.

2.22

子曰："人而无信，不知其可也。大车无輗，小车无軏，其何以行之哉？"

增加的，是可以知道的；周朝又继承了商朝的礼制，所减少的和增加的，可以知道；将来如有继承周朝的礼仪制度，其基本内容不过增增减减，即使传下一百代之久，也是可以推知的。"

【注释】
1 世：古时称三十年为一世。这里指朝代。
2 殷：就是商朝。商朝传至盘庚（商汤王的第九代孙），从奄（今山东省曲阜市）迁都于殷（今河南省安阳县西北），遂称殷。商是国名，殷是国都之名。因：因袭，沿袭。礼：指整个礼仪制度，是规范社会行为的法则、规范、仪式的总称。
3 损益：减少和增加。

【英译文】
Zi Zhang asked whether the state of things ten generations hence could be foretold. The Master said, We know in what ways the Yin Dynasty modified ritual when they followed upon the Xia Dynasty. We know in what ways the Zhou Dynasty modified ritual when they followed upon the Yin. And hence we can foretell what the successors of Zhou Dynasty will be like, even supposing they do not appear till a hundred generations from now.

2.24

子曰："非其鬼而祭之¹，谄也。见义不为，无勇也。"

论语意解

【中译文】
孔子说："一个人不讲信用，那怎么可以呢？如果大车小车上没有横木销子，它靠什么行走呢？"

【注释】
1 信：讲信用。
2 輗（ní）：古代大车（用牛拉，以载重）车辕前面横木上楔嵌的起关联固定作用的木销子（榫头）。
3 軏（yuè）：古代小车（用马拉，以载人）车辕前面横木上楔嵌的起关联固定任用的木销子（榫头）。
4 何以：以何，用什么，靠什么。

【英译文】
The Master (Confucius) said, I do not see what use a man can be put to, whose word cannot be trusted. How can a waggon be made to go if it has no yoke-bar or a carriage, if it has no collar-bar?

2.23

子张问："十世可知也¹？"子曰："殷因于夏礼²，所损益³，可知也；周因于殷礼，所损益，可知也；其或继周者，虽百世，可知也。"

【中译文】
子张问："今后十个朝代礼仪制度的事，可以推知吗？"孔子说："商朝继承了夏朝的礼制，所减少的和

论语意解

2.22

子曰："人而无信，不知其可也。大车无輗，小车无軏，其何以行之哉？"

【注释】

1. 信：讲信用。
2. 輗(ní)：古代大车（用牛拉，以载重）车辕前面横木上驾牲口起关键固定作用的木销子（榫头）。
3. 軏(yuè)：古代小车（用马拉，以载人）车辕前面横木上驾牲口起关键固定作用的木销子（榫头）。
4. 何以：以何，用什么，凭什么。

【英译文】

The Master (Confucius) said, I do not see what use a man can be put to, whose word cannot be trusted. How can a waggon be made to go if it has no yoke-bar or a carriage, if it has no collar-bar?

2.23

子张问："十世可知也？"子曰："殷因于夏礼，所损益，可知也；周因于殷礼，所损益，可知也；其或继周者，虽百世，可知也。"

【注释】

1. 世：古时称三十年为一世。这里指朝代。
2. 殷：就是商朝。商朝传至盘庚（商汤王的第九代孙）从亳（今山东省曲阜市）迁都于殷（今河南省安阳县西北），遂称殷。商是国名，殷是国都之名。因此，殷商连称。
3. 礼：指整个礼仪制度，是规范社会行为的准则、规范，仪式的总称。
4. 损益：减少和增加。

【英译文】

Zi Zhang asked whether the state of things ten generations hence could be foretold. The Master said, We know in what ways the Yin Dynasty modified ritual when they followed upon the Xia Dynasty. We know in what ways the Zhou Dynasty modified ritual when they followed upon the Yin. And hence we can foretell what the successors of Zhou Dynasty will be like, even supposing they do not appear till a hundred generations from now.

2.24

子曰："非其鬼而祭之，谄也。见义不为，无勇也。"

【中译文】

孔子说："一个人不讲信用，那怎么可以呢？如果大车小车上没有横木销子，它靠什么走呢？"

【中译文】

子张问："今后十个朝代礼仪制度的事，可以推知吗？"孔子说："商朝继承了夏朝的礼制，那减少和增加的，是可以知道的；周朝又继承了商朝的礼制，那减少和增加的，是可以知道的；将来如有继承周朝的礼仪制度，其基本内容不过增减变易，即使传下一百代之久，也是可以推知的。"

论语意解

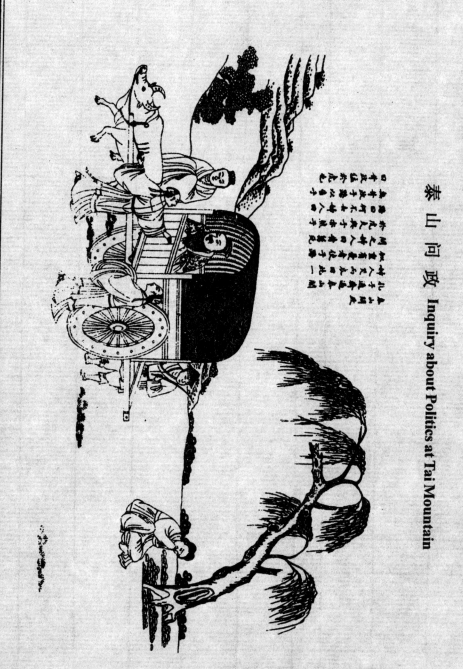

泰山问政 Inquiry about Politics at Tai Mountain

【中译文】

孔子说:"不是自己的祖先却去祭祀它,是谄媚。遇到符合正义的事而不去做,是缺乏勇气。"

【注释】

1 鬼:这里指死去的祖先。

【英译文】

The Master (Confucius) said, It is flattery to offer sacrifices to the dead who don't belong to your own family. It is cowardice to fail to do what is justice.

论语意图

秦司寇处问政于泰山
Inquiry about politics at Tai Mountain

【中译文】

孔子说："不是自己的祖先却去祭祀它，是谄媚。遇到符合正义的事而不去做，是缺乏勇气。"

【注释】

1. 鬼：这里指死去的祖先。

【英译文】

The Master (Confucius) said, It is flattery to offer sacrifices to the dead who don't belong to your own family. It is cowardice to fail to do what is justice.

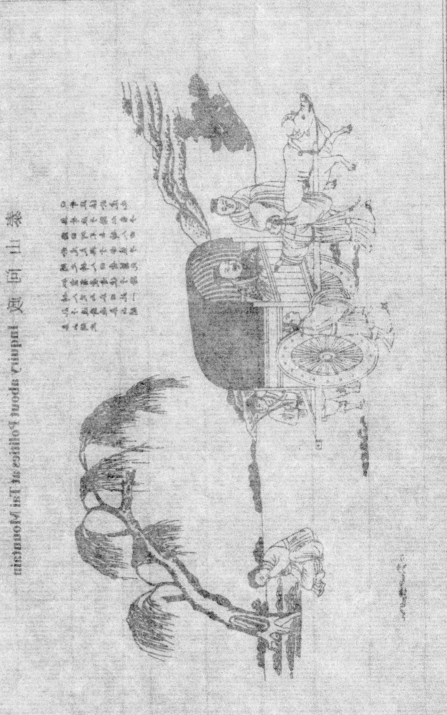

【英译文】

The Master (Confucius) talked about the head of the Ji family, saying, he had eight teams of dancers performing in his courtyard, If this man can be endured, who cannot be endured!

3.2

三家者[1]，以《雍》彻[2]。子曰："相维辟公，天子穆穆[3]，奚取于三家之堂[4]？"

【中译文】

三家大夫祭祖完毕时，让乐工唱着《雍》诗撤掉祭品。孔子说："《雍》诗上说：'协助祭祀的是四方诸侯，天子才是庄严肃穆的主祭者。'这如何能用在三家大夫的庙堂上？

【注释】

1 三家：春秋后期掌握鲁国政权的三家贵族：孟孙氏（即仲孙氏），叔孙氏，季孙氏。他们是鲁桓公之子仲庆父（亦称孟氏）、叔牙、季友的后裔，又称"三桓"。在这三家中，以季孙氏势力最大。他们自恃有政治经济的实力，所以经常有越轨周礼的行为，多次受到孔子的批判。

2 雍：《诗经·周颂》中的一篇。古代，天子祭祀宗庙的仪式举行完毕后，在撤去祭品收拾礼器的时候，专门唱这首诗。亦作"雝"。彻：同"撤"。撤除，拿掉。

论语意解

四三〇九

八佾篇第三（共二十六章）

On Ritural

3.1

孔子谓季氏[1]，八佾舞于庭[2]，是可忍也，孰不可忍也[3]。

【中译文】

孔子谈论季氏，说他在私庭演奏冒用天子规格的乐舞。这种事如果可以容忍，那还有什么不可以容忍的事呢？

【注释】

1 季氏：鲁国正卿季孙氏。此指季平子，即季孙意如。一说，季桓子。

2 八佾："佾（yì）"，行，列。特指古代奏乐舞蹈的行列。一佾，是八个人的行列；八佾，就是八八六十四个人。按周礼规定，天子的乐舞，才可用八佾。诸侯，用六佾；卿、大夫，用四佾；士，用二佾。按季氏的官职，只有用四佾的资格，但他擅自僭（jiàn。超越本分）用了天子乐舞规格的八佾，这是不可饶恕的越轨行为。

3 "是可"句："忍"，容忍。"孰"，疑问代词。什么。一说，"忍"，忍心。

八佾篇第三 （共二十六章）

On Ritual

3.1

孔子谓季氏[1]，「八佾[2]舞于庭，是可忍也[3]，孰不可忍也？」

【英译文】

The Master (Confucius) talked about the head of the Ji family, saying, he had eight teams of dancers performing in his courtyard. If this man can be endured, who cannot be endured?

【中译文】

孔子谈论季氏，说他竟用天子规格的乐舞用天子规格的乐舞……这种事如果可以容忍，那还有什么不可以容忍呢？

【注释】

1 季氏：鲁国正卿季孙氏，此指季平子，即季孙意如。一说，季桓子。

2 八佾：「佾（yì）」，行，列。指排列成行来表演歌舞的乐队。一佾，即八个人的行列。八佾，就是八八六十四个人。按照礼的规定，天子的乐舞，才可用八佾；诸侯用六佾；卿、大夫，用四佾；士，用二佾。按季氏的身份，只有用四佾的资格，他却用了八（jíun）一想用八佾的规模的乐舞，这是不合礼制的越轨行为。

3 是可忍：句中「忍」字，含「忍心」「残忍」之意。一说，「忍」含「容忍」「容忍」之心。

3.2

三家者[1]，以《雍》[2]彻。子曰：「相维辟公，天子穆穆」，奚取于三家之堂？

【中译文】

三家大夫祭祖完毕，也像天子一样唱着《雍》诗撤除祭品。孔子说：「《雍》诗上说：『助祭的是四方诸侯，天子庄严肃穆地主祭。』这如何能用在三家大夫的庙堂上？」

【注释】

1 三家：春秋后期掌握鲁国政权的三家贵族：孟孙氏（即仲孙氏）、叔孙氏、季孙氏，他们都是鲁桓公之子仲庆父（亦称孟氏）的后裔，又称「三桓」。在这三家中，以季孙氏势力最大，他们自持有政治经济实力，原以经常有越轨擅国的行为，多次受到孔子的批判。

2 雍：《诗经·周颂》中的一篇。古代，天子祭宗庙完毕及举行祭毕后，在撤走祭品收拾祭器的时候，奏唱这首诗。引文即这首诗。「彻」同「撤」，撤除祭品。

【英译文】

The Master (Confucius) said, A man who is not Good, what can he have to do with ritual? A man who is not Good, what can he have to do with music?

3.4

林放问礼之本[1]。子曰:"大哉问!礼,与其奢也[2],宁俭;丧,与其易也[3],宁戚。"

【中译文】

林放问礼的根本是什么。孔子说:"你提的问题意义重大啊!从礼仪来说,与其奢侈,不如节俭;从治丧来说,与其隆重而完备,不如真正悲伤。"

【注释】

1 林放:姓林,名放,字子上。鲁国人。一说,孔子的弟子。

2 与其:连词。在比较两件事的利害得失而决定取舍的时候,"与其"用在放弃的一面。后面常用"毋宁"、"不如"、"宁"相呼应。

3 易:本义是把土地整治得平坦。在这里指周到地治办丧葬的礼节仪式。

4 戚:心中悲哀。

【英译文】

Lin Fang asked for some main principles in connection with rites. The Master

---

3 "相维"句:《诗经·周颂·雍》中的句子。"相(xiàng)",本指协助,帮助。这里指傧相,助祭者。"维",助词,没有意义。"辟(bì)",本指君王。这里的"辟公",指诸侯。"穆穆",庄严肃静。形容至美至敬。

4 奚:何,怎么,为什么。堂:祭祀先祖或接待宾客的庙堂。

【英译文】

The Three Families used the Yung Song during the removal of the sacrificial vessels. The Master said, By rulers and lords attended, The Son of Heaven, mysterious- What possible application can such words have in the hall of the Three Families?

3.3

子曰:"人而不仁,如礼何[1]?人而不仁,如乐何?"

【中译文】

孔子说:"一个人不讲仁德,怎么谈礼呢?一个人不讲仁德,怎么谈乐呢?"

【注释】

1 如礼何:"如……何"是古代常用句式,当中一般插入代词、名词或其他词语,意思是"把(对)……怎么样(怎么办)"。

论语意解

四二 四一

【英译文】

The Master (Confucius) said, A man who is not Good, what can he have to do with ritual? A man who is not Good, what can he have to do with music?

3.4

林放问礼之本。子曰："大哉问！礼，与其奢也，宁俭；丧，与其易也，宁戚。"

【中译文】

林放问礼的根本是什么。孔子说："你提的问题意义重大啊！从礼仪来说，与其奢侈，不如节俭；从丧事来说，与其仪式周全完备，不如真正悲痛。"

【注释】

1 林放：姓林，名放，字子丘，曾国人。一说，孔子的弟子。

2 与其：连词，在比较两件事的利害得失而决定取舍时，"与其"用在放弃的一面，后面常用"宁"、"不如"、"宁可"相呼应。

3 易：本义是治理土地整治和平田，引这里指周到和铺张隆重的礼节仪文。

4 戚：心中悲哀。

【英译文】

Lin Fang asked for some main principles in connection with rites. The Master

---

3 "相维辟公"句：《诗经·周颂·雍》中的句子。"相"（xiàng），"本指帮助、辅助"，这里指傧相，助祭者。"维"，助词，无意义。"辟（bì）公"，指诸侯。"穆穆"，庄严肃穆。形容态容齐美至德。

4 奚：何。 忍：忍心。 堂：祭祀之祖庙祭祖核礼，容祖庙堂。

【英译文】

The Three Families used the Yung Song during the removal of the sacrificial vessels. The Master said, By rulers and lords attended, The Son of Heaven, mysterious - What possible application can such words have in the hall of the Three Families?

3.3

子曰："人而不仁，如礼何？人而不仁，如乐何？"

【中译文】

孔子说："一个人不讲仁德，怎么对待礼呢？一个人不讲仁德，怎么对待乐呢？"

【注释】

1 如礼何："如……何"是古代常用句式，当中一般插入代词、名词或其他词语，意思是"把（对）……怎么样（怎么办）"。

3.6

季氏旅于泰山[1]。子谓冉有曰[2]："女弗能救与[3]？"对曰："不能。"子曰："呜呼！曾谓泰山不如林放乎[4]？"

【中译文】

季氏去祭祀泰山。孔子对冉有说："你不能阻止此事吗？"冉有回答说："不能。"孔子说："啊呀！莫非说泰山之神还不如鲁国人林放懂礼吗？"

【注释】

1 旅：古代，祭祀山川叫"旅"。泰山：在今山东省泰安市。按周礼规定，天子才有资格祭祀天下名山大川，诸侯只有资格祭祀在其封地境内的名山大川。季康子不过是鲁国的大夫，却去祭祀泰山，这是越礼行为。

2 冉有：姓冉，名求，字子有，也称冉有。鲁国人，仲弓之族。孔子的弟子，比孔子小二十九岁，生于公元前522年，卒年不详。冉有当时是季康子的家臣。

3 女：同"汝"。你。弗：不。救：补救，劝阻，设法匡正。与：同"欤"。语气词。

4 曾：副词。莫非，难道，竟然。

---

said, A very big question! In ritual at large it is a safe rule always to be too sparing rather than too lavish; and in the particular case of mourning-rites, it would be better to exhibit more grief than to pay too much attention to ceremonies.

3.5

子曰："夷狄之有君[1]，不如诸夏之亡也[2]。"

【中译文】

孔子说："夷狄尚且有君主，不像中原诸国有的没有。"

【注释】

1 夷：我国古代东方少数民族。狄：我国古代北方少数民族。

2 诸夏：当时中原黄河流域华夏族居住的各个诸侯国。亡：同"无"。鲁国的昭公、哀公，都曾逃往国外，形成某一时期内鲁国无国君的现象。由此，孔子发出感叹。此处指中原诸国僭乱、反失了君臣上下之份。

【英译文】

The Master (Confucius) said, The barbarians of the East and North have retained their princes, but with no rites, China is still preferable to these states even without a recognized ruler.

【英译文】

The head of the Ji family was going to make the offerings on Mount Tai. The Master said to Ran You Cannot you save him from this? Ran You replied, I cannot, The Master said, Alas, we can hardly suppose Mount Tai to be ignorant of matters that even Lin Fang enquires into!

3.7

子曰："君子无所争。必也射乎¹！揖让而升²，下而饮。其争也君子。"

【中译文】

孔子说："君子之间没有可争的事。如果有，那一定是射箭比赛吧！就算是射箭，也是互相作揖，谦让，然后登堂；射箭比赛完了走下堂来，互相敬酒。这种争，也是君子之争。"

【注释】

1 射：本是射箭。此指射礼——按周礼所规定的射箭比赛。有四种：一、大射（天子，诸侯，卿，大夫，选属下善射之士而升进使用）。二、宾射（贵族之间，朝见聘会时用）。三、燕射（贵族平时娱乐之用）。四、乡射（民间习射艺）。
2 揖：作揖。拱手行礼，以表尊敬。

论语意解

【英译文】

The Master (Confucius) said, Gentlemen never compete. You will say that in archery they do so. But even then they bow and make way for each other when they are going up to the archery-ground, when they are coming down and at the subsequent drinkingbout. Thus even when competing, they remain gentlemen.

3.8

子夏问曰："'巧笑倩兮¹，美目盼兮²，素以为绚兮³。'何谓也？"子曰："绘事后素⁴。"曰："礼后乎？"子曰："起予者商也⁵！始可可言《诗》已矣。"

【中译文】

子夏问道："'美好的笑容真好看啊，美丽的眼睛左右顾盼啊，粉白的脸庞着色化妆绚丽多彩。'是什么意思呢？"孔子说："先有了白底子，然后才画上画。"子夏又问："礼仪相较仁德是不是在后呢？"孔子说："能阐明我的意思的是你卜商啊！现在开始可以同你谈论《诗》了。"

【注释】

1 巧笑：美好的笑容。倩（qiàn）：指笑时面容格外妍美，笑容好看。兮：助词，啊，呀。
2 盼：眼珠黑白分明，转动灵活。

论语意解

3.7

【原文】

子曰："君子无所争。必也射乎！揖让而升，下而饮，其争也君子。"

【中译文】

孔子说："君子之间没有什么可争的事。如果有，那一定是射箭比赛吧！即使是射箭，也是互相作揖，谦让后登堂；射箭比赛完了走下堂来，互相敬酒。这种争，也是君子之争。"

【注释】

1. 揖：拱手礼简。此指揖礼——按周礼规定的射箭比赛，有四种：一、大射（天子、诸侯、卿、大夫，选属下善射之士而用之）。二、宾射（朝见聘会时用）。三、燕射（贵族平时娱乐之用）。四、乡射（民间习射艺）。
2. 揖：拱手行礼，以示尊敬。

【英译文】

The head of the Ji family was going to make the offerings on Mount Tai. The Master said to Ran You Cannot you save him from this? Ran You replied, I cannot. The Master said, Alas, we can hardly suppose Mount Tai to be ignorant of matters that even Lin Fang enquires into!

3.8

【原文】

子夏问曰："'巧笑倩兮，美目盼兮，素以为绚兮'。何谓也？"子曰："绘事后素。"曰："礼后乎？"子曰："起予者商也！始可与言《诗》已矣。"

【中译文】

子夏问道："'美好的笑容真妩媚啊，美丽的眼睛左右顾盼啊，将白的脂底着色化妆成美丽而多彩'，是什么意思呢？"孔子说："先有了白底子，然后才画上画。"子夏又问："礼仪相较仁德是不是在后呢？"孔子说："能阐明我的意思的是卜商啊！现在才开始可以同你谈论《诗》了。"

【注释】

1. 巧笑：美好的笑容。倩(qiàn)：指笑时面容姿格妩媚美。笑容好看。兮：助词，啊，呀。
2. 盼：眼珠黑白分明，转动灵活。

礼，我能说出来，但是，殷的后代宋国现在施行的礼仪却不足以作为考证的证明。因为文字资料不足，熟悉夏礼、殷礼的贤人也不多。如果典籍资料足够的话，我就能用它来作考证的证明了。"

【注释】

1 杞（qǐ）：古国，现在河南省杞县一带。杞国的君主是夏朝禹的后代。征：证明，引以为证。
2 宋：古国，现在河南省商丘市南部一带。宋国的君主是商朝汤的后代。
3 文：指历史文字资料。献：指贤人。古代，朝廷称德才兼备的贤人为"献臣"。

【英译文】

The Master (Confucius) said, How can we talk about the ritual of the Xia Dynasty? The state of Qi supplies no adequate evidence. How can we talk about the ritual of Yin Dynasty? The state of Song supplies no adequate evidence. For there is a lack both of documents and of learned men. But for this lack we should be able to obtain evidence from these two States.

3.10

子曰："禘自既灌而往者¹，吾不欲观之矣²。"

【中译文】

孔子说："祭之礼，从第一次的献酒之后，我就不想再看下去了。"

3 绚：有文彩，绚丽多彩。"巧笑"二句，见《诗经·卫风·硕人》篇。"素以为绚兮"，不见于现在通行的《毛诗》，可能是佚句。
4 绘事后素："绘事"，画画。"后"，后于，在……之后。"素"，白底子。意思说：画画总是先有个白底子，然后才能画。一说，女子先用素粉敷面，然后才用胭脂、青黛等着色，打扮得漂亮。
5 起：发挥，阐明。予：我。商：卜商，即子夏。

【英译文】

Zi Xia asked, What is the meaning of the following lines from The Book of Poetry: Oh the sweet smile dimpling, The lovely eyes so black and white! Plain silk that you would take for coloured stuff. The Master said, The painting comes after the plain groundwork. Tzu-hsia said, Then ritual comes afterwards? The Master said, Shang it is who bears me up. Finally I have someone with whom I can discuss the Songs!

3.9

子曰："夏礼，吾能言之，杞不足征也¹；殷礼，吾能言之，宋不足征也²。文献不足故也³。足，则吾能征之矣。"

【中译文】

孔子说："夏礼，我能说出来，不过，夏的后代杞国现在施行的礼仪却不足以作为考证的证明；殷代的

【注释】

1 禘(dì)：古代只有天子才可以举行的祭祀祖先的隆重典礼。既：已经。灌：禘礼初始即举行的献酒降神仪式。古代祭祀祖先，一般用活人坐在灵位前象征受祭者（这个人叫"尸"）。煮香草为"郁"，合黍酿成气味芬芳的一种酒"郁鬯（chàng）"。将"郁鬯"献于"尸"前，使其闻一闻酒的香气而并不饮用，然后将酒浇在地上。这整个过程就叫"灌"。

2 不欲观：不愿看，看不下去了。鲁国是周公旦的封地。据《礼记》记载，周公死后，他的侄儿周成王（姬诵）为了追念周公辅佐治国的伟大功勋，特许周公的后代在祭祀时举行最高规格的"禘礼"。但这毕竟是不合礼的。而且，一般在经过"灌"的仪式以后，鲁国的君臣往往也都表现懈怠而无诚意了。所以，孔子说了"不欲观"的话。

【英译文】

The Master (Confucius) said, At the Ancestral Sacrifice, as for all that comes after the libation, I had far rather not witness it!

3.11

或问禘之说。子曰："不知也[1]。知其说者之于天下也，其如示诸斯乎[2]！"指其掌。

论语意解

【中译文】

有人问起举行"祭"的来由。孔子说："不知道。能懂这种道理的人治理整个天下，会像把东西摆在这里一样容易吧！"孔子边说边指着自己的手掌。

【注释】

1 不知也：孔子对鲁国"禘祭"不满，所以，他故意避讳，说不知道"禘祭"的道理。

2 "其如"句："示"，同"置"。摆，放。"诸"，"之于"的合音。"斯"，这。指手掌。这句话的意思是：像把东西摆在掌中一样明白而容易。一说，"示"，同"视"。

【英译文】

Someone asked for an explanation of the Ancestral Sacrifice. The Master said, I do not know. Anyone who knows the explanation can deal with all things under Heaven as easily as he lays things here; and be lays his finger upon the palm of his hand.

3.12

祭如在，祭神如神在。子曰："吾不与祭[1]，如不祭。"

【中译文】

祭祀祖先就好像祖先真在那里，祭祀鬼神就如同鬼神真在那里。孔子说："我如果不亲自参加祭祀，那

论语意释

【中文】

有人问孔子关于"禘"的来由。孔子说:"不知道。懂得这种道理的人治理天下,会像把东西摆在这里一样容易吧!"孔子边说边指着自己的手掌。

【注释】

1 不知也：孔子对鲁国"禘祭"不满，所以他故意避讳，说不知道"禘祭"的道理。
2 其如……：句式，"其"，语气词，放在"于"的合音。"视"，同"示"。指手掌，这句话的意思是：像把东西摆在掌中一样明白而容易。"诸"，"之于"的合音。"示"，同"视"。

【英译文】

Someone asked for an explanation of the Ancestral Sacrifice. The Master said, I do not know. Anyone who knows the explanation can deal with all things under Heaven as easily as he lays his finger upon the palm of his hand.

3.12

祭如在，祭神如神在。子曰："吾不与祭，如不祭。"

【中译文】

祭祀祖先就像祖先真的在那里，祭祀神就如同使神真的在那里。孔子说："我如果不亲自参加祭祀，雅……"

【中译文】

【注释】

1 禘(dì)：古代只有天子才可以举行的祭祀祖先的隆重典礼。礿：古祭名。禘：称祭礼初始即本坊的酿酒最早神位之先。古代祭祀和祖先，一般由活着的人坐在前位的受祭者（这个人叫"尸"，"尸"，"祖曹"——即后裴的"神位"）——和酒，"祼"（dràng）"祼"，然后把酒洒在地上，这整个过程叫做"祼"。

2 不欲观：不愿看。春水下去了。鲁国是周公的旧地，据《礼记》记载，周公死后，他的儿子周成王（诵诵）为了追念周公辅佐治国的伟大功勋，特许周公后代在祭祀时用举行最高规格的"禘礼"，如以当礼不合礼的。而且，一般在经过了"禘"，即以后，曾因册封群臣在往往稀疏表现懈意而不诚意了。所以，孔子说下了的"不欲观"的话。

【英译文】

The Master (Confucius) said, At the Ancestral Sacrifice, as for all that comes after the libation, I had far rather not witness it!

3.11

百姓所说的"灶王爷"。旧俗，阴历腊月二十三（或二十四）日烧纸马，供奉饴糖，送灶神上天，谓之"送灶"；腊月三十日（除夕），又迎回来，谓之"迎灶"。灶神地位虽较低，但上可通天，决定人的祸福，故当时人们的俗话才说"宁媚于灶"：祭祀神明时首先要奉 承巴结的是灶神。

【英译文】

Wang Sunjia asked about the meaning of the saying, better pay court to the stove than pay court to the Shrine. The Master said, It is not true. He who has put himself in the wrong with Heaven has no means of expiation left.

3.14

子曰："周监于二代[1]，郁郁乎文哉[2]！吾从周 。"

【中译文】

孔子说："周朝的礼乐制度等是借鉴于夏商两代而发展起来的，多么博雅丰盛啊！我尊从周代的礼乐制度。"

【注释】

1 监：通"鉴"。本义是镜子。引申为照，考察，可以作为警戒或引为教训的事。在这里是借鉴于前代的意思。二代：指夏、商两个朝代。

就如同不祭祀一样。"

【注释】

1 与：参与，参予，参加。

【英译文】

Of the saying, 'The word¡°sacrifice¡±is like the word ¡°present¡±; one should sacrifice to a spirit as though that spirit was present', the Master said, If I am not present at the sacrifice, it is as though there were no sacrifice.

3.13

王孙贾问曰[1]："与其媚于奥[2]，宁媚于灶[3]。何谓也？"子曰："不然。获罪于天，无所祷也 。"

【中译文】

王孙贾问"人们说与其奉承奥神，不如巴结灶神。这话怎么讲？"孔子说："不对。如果得罪了天，向谁祈祷都是没有用的。"

【注释】

1 王孙贾：卫灵公时卫国的大夫，有实权。
2 媚：谄媚，巴结。奥：本义指室内的西南角。这里指屋内西南角的神。古时尊长居西南，所以奥神的地位应比灶神尊贵些。
3 灶：本义是炉灶，用来烹煮食物或烧水。从夏代就以灶为神，称"灶君"，为"五祀之一"，即老

论语意解

祭如何不祭和一样。

【注释】

1 与：参与，参加。

【英译文】

Of the saying, 'The word sacrifice is like the word present': one should sacrifice to a spirit as though that spirit was present, the Master said, 'If I am not present at the sacrifice, it is as though there were no sacrifice.'

3.13

王孙贾问曰：“与其媚于奥，宁媚于灶，何谓也？”子曰：“不然。获罪于天，无所祷也。”

【中译文】

王孙贾问：“人们都说与其奉承奥神，不如巴结灶神，这话怎么讲？”孔子说：“不对。如果得罪了天，向谁祈祷都是没用的。”

【注释】

1 王孙贾：卫灵公时卫国的大夫，有实权。

2 奥：深处，引申为室内。本文指室内的西南角。古时室内的西南角，被认为是神的所居处以及尊贵者所居之处。

3 灶：本义是煮饭用的灶。用来供奉灶神就成灶。从灶代祭，...以灶为神。故“灶神”为“五祀之一”，即名...

【英译文】

Wang Sunjia asked about the meaning of the saying, better pay court to the stove than pay court to the Shrine. The Master said, It is not true. He who has put himself in the wrong with Heaven has no means of expiation left.

3.14

子曰：“周监于二代，郁郁乎文哉！吾从周。”

【中译文】

孔子说：“周朝的礼仪制度是借鉴于夏商两代而发展来的，多么丰富多采啊！我遵从周代的礼仪制度。”

【注释】

1 监：通“鉴”，引申为照耀、考察，在这里是借鉴参照的意思。

2 二代：指夏、商两个朝代。

2 郁郁：原意是草木丰盛茂密的样子，也指香气浓厚。这里指繁盛，完美丰富多彩，文采显著。

【英译文】

The Master (Confucius) said, Chou could survey the two preceding dynasties. What a great wealth of culture! I would follow upon the rituals of Chou.

3.15

子入太庙[1]，每事问。或曰："孰谓鄹人之子知礼乎[2]？入太庙，每事问。"子闻之，曰："是礼也。"

【中译文】

孔子进入太庙，对每件事都要询问，有人说："谁说鄹邑人的儿子懂礼呢？进入太庙，每件事都要问一问。"孔子听后，说："这样做，就是礼啊。"

【注释】

1 太庙：古代指供奉祭祀君主祖先的庙。开国的君主叫太祖，太祖的庙叫太庙。因为周公（姬旦）是鲁国最初受封的君主，所以，当时鲁国的太庙，就是周公庙。

2 孰谓：谁说。鄹(zōu)：又写为"陬"，"郰"。春秋时鲁国的邑名，在今山东省曲阜市东南一带。孔

子的父亲叔梁纥（hé）在鄹邑做过大夫。"鄹人"，指叔梁纥。"鄹人之子"，即指孔子。

【英译文】

When the Master entered the Grand Temple he asked questions about everything there. Someone said, Do not tell me that this son of a villager from Shu Liang he father of Confucius is expert in matters of ritual. When he went to the Grand Temple, he had to ask about everything. The master hearing of this said, Just so! Such is the ritual.

3.16

子曰："射不主皮[1]，为力不同科[2]，古之道也。"

【中译文】

孔子说："射箭不在于要射穿那皮靶子，因为各个人的力气大小有所不同，自古以来规矩就是如此。"

【注释】

1 射不主皮："射"，射箭。周代仪礼制度中有专门为演习礼乐而举行的射箭比赛，称"射礼"。这里的"射"即指此。"皮"，指用兽皮做成的箭靶子。古代，箭靶子叫"侯"，用布做或用皮做。《仪礼·乡射礼》："礼射不主皮。"射礼比赛，射箭应当以是否"中的"为主，而不在于用力去射，把皮靶子穿透。这与作战比武的"军射"不同。那是提倡

【英译文】

When the Master entered the Grand Temple he asked questions about everything there. Someone said, Do not tell me that this son of a villager from Shu Liang he father of Confucius is expert in matters of ritual. What he went to the Grand Temple, he had to ask about everything. The master hearing of this said. Just so! Such is the ritual.

3.16

子曰："射不主皮，为力不同科，古之道也。"

【中译文】

孔子说："射箭不在于射穿那张皮做的箭靶子，因为各个人的力气大小有所不同，自古以来规矩就是如此。"

【注释】

1 射不主皮："射"，射箭，射礼。"皮"，这里指……

2 ……

【英译文】

The Master (Confucius) said, Chou could survey the two preceding dynasties. What a great wealth of culture! I would follow upon the rituals of Chou.

3.15

子入太庙，每事问。或曰："孰谓鄹人之子知礼乎？入太庙，每事问。"子闻之，曰："是礼也。"

【中译文】

孔子进入太庙，每件事情都要请教问问，有人说："谁说那个鄹邑人的儿子懂礼呢？进入太庙，每件事情都问一问。"孔子听了，说："这样就是礼呀。"

【注释】

1 太庙：古代指供奉君主先祖的庙堂。开国的君主叫太祖，太祖的庙叫太庙。因为鲁国的国君……是最初受封的君主，所以，当时鲁国的太庙就是周公庙。

2 鄹……鄹(zōu)……

【英译文】

Zi Gong wanted to do away with the presentation of a sacrificial sheep at the announcement of each new moon. The Master said, Zi Gong You grudge sheep, but I grudge ritual.

3.18

子曰："事君尽礼[1]，人以为谄也[2]。"

【中译文】

孔子说："事奉君主，完全按照礼制的规定，别人却以为这样做是对君主谄媚。"

【注释】

1 事：事奉，服务于。

2 谄（chǎn）：谄媚，用卑贱的态度向人讨好，奉承。

【英译文】

The Master (Confucius) said, Were anyone to serve his prince according to the full prescriptions of ritual, he would be thought a flatterer.

3.19

定公问[1]："君使臣[2]，臣事君，如之何[3]？"孔子对曰："君使臣以礼，臣事君以忠。"

论语意解

用力射的，有"射甲彻七札（穿透甲革七层）"之说。

2 力：指每个人天生的力气。科：指等级，类别。

【英译文】

The Master (Confucius) said, In archery it is not the hide that counts, for some men have more strength than others. This is the way of the Ancients.

3.17

子贡欲去告朔之饩羊[1]。子曰："赐也！尔爱其羊[2]，我爱其礼。"

【中译文】

子贡想把每月初一祭祀需宰杀的羊节省下来。孔子说："赐呀！你爱惜的是那头羊，我爱惜的却是那种礼仪。"

【注释】

1 告朔：阴历的每月初一，叫"朔"。古代制度，诸侯在每月的初一来到祖庙，杀一只活羊举行祭礼，表示每月"听政"的开始，叫"告朔"。其实，在当时的鲁国，君主已不亲自到祖庙去举行"告朔"礼了。饩（xì）：活的牲畜。

2 尔：代词。你。

【英译文】

The Master (Confucius) said, In archery it is not the hide that counts, for some men have more strength than others. This is the way of the Ancients.

3.17

子贡欲去告朔之饩羊。子曰："赐也！尔爱其羊，我爱其礼。"

【中译文】

子贡想把每月初一告朔祭祖用的羊去掉不用。孔子说："赐呀！你爱惜的是那只羊，我爱惜的是那种礼。"

【注释】

1 告朔：阴历每月初一日叫"朔"，叫"告朔"。古代制度，每年年底周天子把第二年一来的规定，将一只活羊供行告朔礼。本来制的月历颁赐各诸侯国，诸侯自己不来亲到祖庙通去举行"告朔"礼，祖到当时的鲁国君。

2 饩(xì)：活的牲畜。

【英译文】

Zi Gong wanted to do away with the presentation of a sacrificial sheep at the announcement of each new moon. The Master said, Zi Gong You grudge sheep, but I grudge ritual.

3.18

子曰："事君尽礼，人以为谄也。"

【中译文】

孔子说："事奉君主，完全按照礼制做的事，别人却以为这样做是对君主谄媚。"

【注释】

1 事：事奉。服务于。

2 谄(chǎn)：谄媚。用卑贱的态度向人讨好；奉承。

【英译文】

The Master (Confucius) said, Were anyone to serve his prince according to the full prescriptions of ritual, he would be thought a flatterer.

3.19

定公问："君使臣，臣事君，如之何？"

孔子对曰："君使臣以礼，臣事君以忠。"

愁而不悲伤。"

【注释】

1 关雎（jū）：《诗经》第一篇的篇名。因它的首句是"关关雎鸠，在河之洲。"故名。"雎鸠"，是古代所说的一种水鸟。"关关"，是雎鸠的鸣叫声。这是一首爱情诗。古代也用这首诗作为对婚礼的祝贺词。淫：放纵，放荡，过分。

【英译文】

The Master (Confucius) said, The Doem Guanjiu pleasure not carried to the point of debauch; grief not carried to the point of self-injury.

3.21

哀公问社于宰我[1]。宰我对曰："夏后氏以松[2]，殷人以柏，周人以栗，曰：使民战栗[3]。"子闻之，曰："成事不说，遂事不谏[4]，既往不咎[5]。"

【中译文】

鲁哀公问宰我，祭祀土地神的神用什么木料做牌位？宰我回答："夏朝人用松树，商朝用柏树，周朝用栗子树。用栗的意思是让老百姓战栗。"孔子听了以后，说："已经做过的事情不要再说了，已经完成的事不必再规劝了，已经过去的事不要再去责备追究了。"

论语意解

五八

五七

【中译文】

鲁定公问："君主使用臣子，臣子事奉君主，应当怎样去做呢？"孔子回答："君主应当靠礼仪使用臣子，臣子应当靠忠诚事奉君主。"

【注释】

1 定公：鲁国的君主，姓姬，名宋，谥号"定"。襄公之子，昭公之弟，继昭公而立。在位十五年（公元前509－前495）。鲁定公时，孔子担任过司寇，代理过宰相。鲁定公的哥哥昭公，曾被贵族季氏赶出国外。因此，鲁定公询问孔子，如何正确处理君臣关系，以维持政权。

2 使：使用。

3 如之何：如何，怎样。"之"是虚词。

【英译文】

Duke Ding asked for a precept concerning a ruler's use of his ministers and a minister's service to his ruler. The Master replied saying, A ruler in employing his ministers should be guided solely by the prescriptions of ritual. Ministers in serving their ruler, solely by devotion to his cause.

3.20

子曰："《关雎》乐而不淫[1]，哀而不伤。"

【中译文】

孔子说："《关雎》诗篇，表现出快乐而不流荡；忧

【英译文】

The Master (Confucius) said The Doem Guanju pleasure not carried to the point of debauch, grief not carried to the point of self-injury.

3.21

【英译文】

Duke Ding asked for a precept concerning a ruler's use of his ministers and a minister's service to his ruler. The Master replied saying, A ruler in employing his ministers should be guided solely by the prescriptions of ritual. Ministers in serving their ruler solely by devotion to his cause

3.20

fear and trembling.' The Master heard of it and said, What is over and done with, one does not discuss. What has already taken its course, one does not criticise; What already belongs to the past, one does not censure.

3.22

子曰："管仲之器小哉[1]！"或曰："管仲俭乎？"曰："管氏有三归[2]，官事不摄[3]，焉得俭[4]？""然则管仲知礼乎？"曰："邦君树塞门[5]，管氏亦树塞门。邦君为两君之好，有反坫[6]，管氏亦有反坫。管氏而知礼，孰不知礼？"

【中译文】

孔子说："管仲的气量真小啊！"有人问："管仲节俭吗？"孔子说："管仲家收取老百姓大量的市租，为他家管事的官员也是一人一职而不兼任，岂能说是节俭？"那人又问："那么，管仲知礼吗？"孔子说："国君在宫殿大门前树立一道影壁短墙，管仲家门口也树立影壁短墙。国君设宴招待别国的君主，举行友好会见时，在堂上专门设置献过酒后放空杯子的土台，管仲家也设置这样的土台。若说管仲知礼，那还有谁不知礼呢？"

【注释】

1 管仲：姓管，名夷吾，字仲。一名管敬仲。齐国姬姓之后人。颍（yǐng）上（今安徽省西北部，淮河北

论语意解

六五〇九

【注释】

1 社：土地神。这里指的是制作代表土地神的木头牌位。宰我：姓宰，名予，字子我。又称宰我。鲁国人。孔子早年的弟子。

2 夏后氏：本是部落名。相传禹是部落领袖。禹的儿子启，建立了我国历史上第一个朝代－－夏朝。后世指夏朝的人，就称"夏后氏"。以：用。松：古人以为神要凭借某种东西才能来享受人对神的祭祀，而把这种所凭借的东西称为"神主"（木制的牌位）。夏代人用松木做土地神的神主。一说，是指栽树以作祭祀。夏代人居住在河东（今山西省西南部），山野适宜栽松树；殷代人居住在北亳（今河南省商丘市以北），山野适宜栽伯树；周代人，居住在酆镐（fēnghào）。今陕西省西安市西北、西南一带），山野适宜栽栗树。

3 战栗：因害怕而发抖，哆嗦。这里，宰我"让老百姓战栗"的解释有牵强之处，孔子不满。

4 遂：已经完成，成功。谏（jiàn）：规劝，使改正错误。

5 咎（jiù）：责备。

【英译文】

Duke Ai asked Zai Wo about the Holy Ground. He replied, The Xia sovereigns marked theirs with a pine, the men of Yin used a cypress, the men of Zhou used a chestnut-tree, saying, 'This will cause the common people to be in

formed no double duties. How can he be cited as an example of frugality? That may be, the other said; but surely he had a great knowledge of ritual? The Master said, Only the ruler of a State may build a screen to mask his gate; but Guan Zhong had such a screen. Only the ruler of a State, when meeting another such ruler, may use cup-mounds; but Guan Zhong used one. If even Guan Zhong is to be cited as an expert in ritual, who is not an expert in ritual?

3.23

子语鲁大师乐[1]，曰："乐其可知也：始作，翕如也[2]；从之[3]，纯如也[4]，皦如也[5]，绎如也[6]，以成。"

【中译文】

孔子对鲁国的乐官谈论关于演奏音乐的过程，说："奏乐的道理是可以知道的：开始时合奏和谐协调；乐曲展开以后，和谐悦耳，节奏分明，又连绵不断，直到乐曲演奏终了。"

【注释】

1 语：动词。对……说。大师："大"，同"太"。"大师"，就是"太师"，是国家主管音乐的官。

2 翕（xī）：和顺，协调。一说，兴奋，热烈。

3 从：通"纵"。放纵，展开。

4 纯：美好，善，佳。

5 皦（jiǎo）：明亮，清晰，音节分明。

6 绎（yì）：连续，连绵不断。

论语意解

六二 六一

岸，颍河下游）人。生年不详，卒于公元前 645 年。春秋初期有名的政治家。帮助齐桓公以"尊王攘夷"相号召，使桓公成为春秋时诸侯中第一个霸主。孔子与管仲的政见不一致，对管仲违背周礼的某些做法，孔子进行了批评。器：气量，度量，胸襟。

2 有三归：指管仲将照例归公的市租据为己有。"三归"，指市租。

3 摄：兼任，兼职。当时，大夫的家臣，都是一人常兼数事。而管仲却是设许多管事的家臣，一人一事一职。

4 焉得：怎么可以，哪能算是。

5 邦君：诸侯，国君。树：树立，建立。塞门："塞"，遮蔽。古代，天子和诸侯，在宫殿大门口筑上一道短墙作为遮蔽物，以区别内外。也称"萧墙"，相当于后世所说的"照壁"，"影壁"。天子的塞门在天门之外，诸侯的塞门在大门之内。

6 反坫："坫（diàn）"，古代设于堂中，供祭祀或宴会时放礼器和酒具的土台子。反坫，是诸侯宴会时的一种礼节。指君主招待别国国君，举行友好会见，献过酒之后，把空杯子放回坫上。

【英译文】

The Master (Confucius) said, Guan Zhong was in reality a man of very narrow capacities. Someone said, Surely he displayed an example of frugality? The Master said, Guan Zhong had three lots of wives, his State officers performed no double duties. How can he be cited as an example of frugality? That may be, the other said, but surely he had a great knowledge of ritual? The Master said, Only the ruler of a State may build a screen to mask his gate; but Guan Zhong had such a screen. Only the ruler of a State, when meeting another such ruler, may use cup-mounds; but Guan Zhong used one. If even Guan Zhong is to be cited as an expert in ritual, who is not an expert in ritual?

3.23

子语鲁太师乐，曰："乐其可知也：始作，翕如也；从之，纯如也，皦如也，绎如也，以成。"

【中译文】

孔子给鲁国的乐官谈论演奏音乐的道理，说："演奏音乐的道理是可以知道的：开始演奏合奏和谐协调，然后放开，声音纯正明朗，又连续不断，一直到演奏完毕了。"

【注释】

1. 语：动词，对……说。太师："太"，同"太"。"太师"，是古代乐工首长的称谓。

2. 翕(xī)：和顺，协调。一说，关合，收敛。

3. 从：通"纵"。放纵，展开。

4. 纯：美好；谐。

5. 皦(jiǎo)：明亮；清晰；音节分明。

6. 绎(yì)：连续，连绵不断。

【英译文】

The Master (Confucius) said, Guan Zhong was in reality a man of very narrow capacities. Someone said, Surely he displayed an example of frugality? The Master said, Guan Zhong had three lots of wives his State officers per...

上蔡县西南)一带，故能与仪地边界的官员见面。

2 斯：代词。这个地方。

3 从者：随从孔子的弟子。

4 二三子：这里是称呼孔子弟子。"二三"，表示约数，犹言"各位"。"子"，对人的尊称。患：担忧，犯愁，担心。丧：失去。这里指孔子失掉 官位，没有官 职。孔子原为鲁国的司寇，后离鲁 去卫，又去陈，政治抱负未能实现。

5 木铎："铎（duó）"，一种金口木舌的大铜铃。古代以召集群众，下通知，宣布政教法令，或在有战事时使用。这里是以"木铎"作比喻，说孔子将能起到为国家发布政令的作用（管理天下）。

【英译文】

The guardian of the frontier-mound at Yi asked to be introduced to the Master, saying, No gentleman arriving at this frontier has ever yet failed to accord me an interview. The Master's followers presented him. On going out the man said, Sirs, you must not be disheartened by his failure. It is now a very long time since the Way prevailed in the world. I feel sure that Heaven intends to use your Master as a guide for the people.

3.25

子谓《韶》[1]："尽美矣[2]，又尽善也[3]。"谓《武》[4]："尽美矣，未尽善也。"

论语意解

【英译文】

When talking with the Grand Master of Lu about music, the Master said, Their music in so far as one can find out about it began with a strict unison. Soon the musicians were given more liberty; but the tone remained harmonious, brilliant, consistent, right on to the end.

3.24

仪封人请见[1]，曰："君子之至于斯也[2]，吾未尝不得见也。"从者见之[3]。出曰："二三子何患于丧乎[4]？天下之无道也，天将以夫子为木铎[5]。"

【中译文】

有一位在仪地防守边界的官员来求见孔子。他说："凡是到这地方来的君子，我从来没有不能见的。"随从孔子的弟子领这官员去见了孔子。出来以后这官员对孔子的弟子们说："你们几位何必担心孔子没有官职呢？天下失去规范很久了，上天必将让你们的老师作为传播正道的人。"

【注释】

1 仪封人："仪"，地名，卫国的一个邑，在今河南省兰考县境内。"封"，边界。仪封人，指在仪这个地方镇守边界的官员。一说，封人仪姓。孔子周游列国，到过陈（今河南省淮阳县）、蔡（今河南省

原文意译

仪封人请见，曰："君子之至于斯也，未尝不得见也。"从者见之。出曰："二三子，何患于丧乎？天下之无道也久矣，天将以夫子为木铎。"

【注释】

1. 仪封人："仪"，地名，卫国的一个邑，在今河南省兰考县境内。"封"，边界。仪封人，镇守这个地方边界的官员。一说，封人位尊，周朝列国，郑封邑（今河南省新郑县）、蔡（今河南省上蔡县西南）一带，故推与仪地边界的官员见面。
2. 斯：代词，这个地方。
3. 从者：随从孔子的弟子。
4. 二三子：这里是称呼孔子弟子。"二三"，未示约数。辞气"各位"，"子"，对人的尊称。患：担忧。
   丧怨：失去。丧，失。这里指带孔子失掉官位。
   没有官位，出：北于原为鲁国的司寇，后离鲁。走孔；义无位，政治抱负未能实现。
5. 木铎："铎(duó)"，一种金口木舌的大铜铃。古代以召集雅众、下达政策，宣布政策法令。要有行政事项时便用。这里是以"木铎"作比喻。说孔子将能能够到国家发布政令的作用。

【英译文】

The guardian of the frontier-mound at Yi asked to be introduced to the Master, saying, No gentleman arriving at this frontier has ever yet failed to accord me an interview. The Master's followers presented him. On going out the man said, Sirs, you must not be disheartened by his failure. It is now a very long time since the Way prevailed in the world. I feel sure that Heaven intends to use your Master as a guide for the people.

3.25

子谓《韶》："尽美矣，又尽善也。"谓《武》："尽美矣，未尽善也。"

【中译文】

有一位仪地防守边界的官员请求来见孔子。他说："凡是到这地方来的君子，我从来没有不能见到的。"随从孔子的弟子便让这位官员去见孔子了。出来以后这位官员对孔子的弟子们说："你们几位何必为孔子没有职位呢？天下失去规范很久了，上天将要借他们老师作为劝导规正道的人。"

【英译文】

When talking with the Grand Master of Lu about music, the Master said Their music in so far as one can find out about it began with a strict unison. Soon the musicians were given more liberty; but the tone retained harmonious, brilliant, consistent, right on to the end.

3.24

仪封人请见了，曰："君子之至于斯也，招， 未尝不得见也。"从者见之。出曰："二三子，何患于丧乎？天下之无道也，天将以夫子为木铎。"

吾何以观之哉！"

【中译文】

孔子说："居于高位，待人不宽厚；举行仪礼时不庄重严肃；参加丧礼时不显示哀戚，我如何能看得下去呢？"

【注释】

1 上：上位，高位。宽：待人宽厚，宽宏大量。

【英译文】

The Master (Confucius) said, High office filled by men of narrow views, ritual performed without reverence, the forms of mourning observed without grief-these are things that I cannot bear to see!

论语意解

【中译文】

孔子谈到《韶》这一乐舞说："美极了啊，又好极了。"谈到《武》这一乐舞说："美极了啊，但还不够好。"

【注释】

1 韶（sháo）：传说上古虞舜时的一组乐舞，也叫"大韶"。古解："韶"就是"绍（继承）"，舞乐主题表现了"舜绍尧之道德"，即指虞舜通过禅让继承帝位，故舞乐中有一种太和之气，可以称为"尽善"。

2 美：指乐舞的艺术形式。音调声容之盛美。

3 善：指乐舞的思想内容，蕴藉内涵之美。

4 武：周代用于祭祀的"六舞"之一，是表现周武王战胜殷纣王的一组音乐和舞蹈，也叫"大武"。古解：武王用武除暴，为天下所乐。《诗经·周颂》中有《武》篇，为武王克殷后作，乃赞颂武王武功的乐舞歌词。孔子认为武王伐纣虽顺应天意民心，但毕竟经过征战，故说"未尽善"。

【英译文】

The Master (Confucius) spoke of the Shao music as being perfect beauty and at the same time perfect goodness; but of the Wu music as being perfect beauty, but not perfect goodness.

3.26

子曰："居上不宽[1]，为礼不敬，临丧不哀，

【中译文】

孔子说："居于高位，待人不宽厚；参加典礼而不恭敬；参加丧礼而不悲哀，我怎么能看得下去呢？"

【注释】

1. 上：上位，高位。宽：待人宽厚，宽宏大量。

【英译文】

The Master (Confucius) said, High office filled by men of narrow views; ritual performed without reverence; the forms of mourning observed without grief: these are things that I cannot bear to see!

【中译文】

孔子谈到《韶》这一乐舞说："美极了，又好极了。"谈到《武》这一乐舞说："美极了，但还不够好。"

【注释】

1. 韶(sháo)：传说上古虞舜时的一种乐舞，也叫"大韶"。古解："韶"就是"绍"(继承)，颂虞舜了，"绍继尧之道德"，即指虞舜继承并发扬尧的帝位，故乐舞中有"神太和之气"，可以称为"尽善"。
2. 美：指乐舞的艺术形式，音调声容之盛美；
3. 善：指乐舞的思想内容，蕴藉内涵之美。
4. 武：周代用于祭祀和乐的"六舞"之一，是歌颂周武王伐纣取代殷纣王的一种乐舞和舞蹈，也叫"大武"。古解：《诗经·周颂》中有《武》篇，歌颂武王克殷定作，乃赞颂武王的功勋业绩而作。孔子以为武王取天下且顺应天意民心，但毕竟经过了征战，故曰"未尽善"。

【英译文】

The Master (Confucius) spoke of the Shao music as being perfect beauty and at the same time perfect goodness; but of the Wu music as being perfect beauty, but not perfect goodness.

里仁篇第四（共二十六章）
On Virtue

4.1

子曰："里仁为美[1]。择不处仁[2]，焉得知[3]？"

【中译文】

孔子说："居住在民风淳厚地方才是美好的。如果不选择好的地方居住，怎能算得上是明智呢？"

【注释】

1 里：邻里。周制，五家为邻，五邻（二十五家）为里。这里用作动词，居住。仁：讲仁德而又风俗淳厚的地方。
2 处：居住，相处。
3 焉：怎么，哪里，哪能。

【英译文】

The Master (Confucius) said, It is virtuous that a man gives to a neighbourhood its beauty. One who is free to choose, yet does not prefer to dwell among the Good—how can he be considered wise?

4.2

子曰："不仁者不可以久处约[1]，不可以长处乐[2]。仁者安仁，知者利仁[3]。"

太庙问礼 Inquiring About Ritual at Tai Temple

Inquiring About A Ritual at Tai Temple

【英译文】

The Master (Confucius) said, 'Only a Good Man knows how to like people, knows how to dislike them.'

4.4

子曰："苟志于仁矣[1]，无恶也[2]。

【中译文】

孔子说："真下决心努力实践仁，那就不会去作恶了。"

【注释】

1 苟：假如，如果。志：立志，决心。

2 恶：坏，坏事。

【英译文】

The Master (Confucius) said, He whose heart is in the smallest degree set upon Goodness will dislike no one.

4.5

子曰："富与贵，是人之所欲也；不以其道得之，不处也[1]。贫与贱，是人之所恶也；不以其道得之，不去也[2]。君子去仁，恶乎成名[3]？君子无终食之间违仁[4]，造次必于是[5]，颠沛必于是[6]。"

【中译文】

孔子说："没有仁德的人，不能长久处于贫困，也不能长久处于安乐之中。有仁德的人才能安心于实行仁德，有智慧的人知道仁德的好处而追求仁德。"

【注释】

1 约：贫困，俭约。

2 乐：安乐，快乐。

3 知：同"智"。

【英译文】

The Master (Confucius) said, Without virtue a man cannot for long endure adversity, cannot for long enjoy prosperity. The Good Man rests content with Goodness; he that is merely wise pursues Goodness in the belief that it pays to do so.

4.3

子曰："唯仁者能好人[1]，能恶人。[2]"

【中译文】

孔子说："只有仁爱之人，才能恰如其分地喜欢或憎恨人。

【注释】

1 好（hào）：喜爱，喜欢。

2 恶（wù）：厌恶，讨厌。

【英译文】

The Master (Confucius) said, 'Only a Good Man knows how to like people, knows how to dislike them.'

4.4

子曰："苟志于仁矣，无恶也。"

【中译文】

孔子说："真正立志实践仁德，那就不会去作恶事了。"

【注释】

1. 苟：服如。如果。志：立志。铭心。
2. 恶：坏。坏事。

【英译文】

The Master (Confucius) said, 'He whose heart is in the smallest degree set upon Goodness will dislike no one.'

4.5

子曰："富与贵，是人之所欲也；不以其道得之，不处也。贫与贱，是人之所恶也；不以其道得之，不去也。君子去仁，恶乎成名？君子无终食之间违仁，造次必于是，颠沛必于是。"

【中译文】

孔子说："有仁德的人，不偏不倚于贫困，也不偏不倚于富贵之中。有仁德的人本着爱心与仁德，对有智慧的人施道仁德以褒贬其是而遏未之傲。"

【注释】

1. 约：穷困，俭约。
2. 乐：安乐，快乐。
3. 利：同"锢"。

【英译文】

The Master (Confucius) said, 'Without virtue a man cannot for long endure adversity, cannot for long enjoy prosperity. The Good Man rests content with Goodness; he that is merely wise pursues Goodness in the belief that it pays to do so.'

4.3

子曰："唯仁者能好人，能恶人。"

【中译文】

孔子说："只有仁德之人，才能够褒贬其是非地喜爱人，憎恨人。"

【注释】

1. 好（hào）：喜爱，喜欢。
2. 恶（wù）：厌恶，讨厌。

but that he cleaves to this; never so tottering but that he cleaves to this.

4.6

子曰："我未见好仁者，恶不仁者。好仁者，无以尚之[1]；恶不仁者，其为仁矣，不使不仁者加乎其身。有能一日用其力于仁矣乎？我未见力不足者。盖有之矣[2]，我未之见也[3]。"

【中译文】

孔子说："我没见过爱好仁德的人，也没见过讨厌不讲仁德的人。爱好仁德的人，是无法超越的；厌恶不讲仁德的人，在实行仁德时，不会让不仁德的人影响自己。有能在一天之内用自己的力量去实行仁德的吗？我还没见过因此而力量不够的。可能会有，可是我没见过。"

【注释】

1 尚：超过、高出。

2 盖：发语词。表示肯定的语气。

3 未之见：未见之。没看到过这种人或这种情况。

【英译文】

The Master (Confucius) said, I have never yet seen one who really cared for Goodness, nor one who really hated wickedness. One who really cared for Goodness would never let any other consideration come first. One who hated

论语意解

【中译文】

孔子说："发财和升官，是人们所向往的，如果不用正当的方法去获得，君子是不接受的。生活穷困和地位卑微，是人们所厌恶的，若不是用正当的方法去摆脱，君子是不会躲避的。君子假如离开仁德，成名有何意义呢？君子一刻也不违背仁。即使是在最紧迫的时刻，或即使是在流离困顿的时候也必须按仁德去做。"

【注释】

1 处：享受，接受。

2 去：避开，摆脱。

3 恶：同"乌"。相当于"何"。疑问副词。怎样，如何。

4 终食之间：吃完一顿饭的工夫。违：违背，离开。

5 造次：紧迫，仓促，急迫。必于是：必须这样做。"是"，代词。这，此。

6 颠沛：本义是跌倒，偃仆。引申为贫困，流离困顿。

【英译文】

Wealth and rank are what everyone desires; but if they can only be retained to the detriment of the Way he professes, he must relinquish them. Poverty and obscurity are what everyone detests; but if they can only be avoided to the detriment of the Way he professes, he must accept them. The gentleman who ever parts company with Goodness does not fulfil that name. Never for a moment does a gentleman quit the way of Goodness. He is never so harried

名句意解

4.5

【中译文】

孔子说："发财和升官，是人们所向往的。如果不用正当的方法去获得，君子是不接受的。贫苦和下贱，是人们所厌恶的，若不是用正当的办法去摆脱，君子是不会去摆脱的。君子一刻也不违背仁德，即使是在最紧迫的时刻，必须这样做，即便是在颠沛流离的时候也必须这样做。"

【注释】

1. 处：享受，接受。
2. 去：摆脱，摒弃。
3. 恶：同"乌"，相当于"何"，疑问副词。怎样，哪里。
4. 终食之间：吃完一顿饭的工夫。比喻短暂。
5. 造次：紧迫，仓促，忽遽。必于是：必须这样做。是，"此同"，这，此。
6. 颠沛：本义是跌倒，偃仆。引申为贫困，流离困顿。

【英译文】

Wealth and rank are what everyone desires; but if they can only be retained to the detriment of the Way he professes, he must relinquish them. Poverty and obscurity are what everyone detests; but if they can only be avoided to the detriment of the Way he professes, he must accept them. The gentleman who ever parts company with Goodness does not fulfil that name. Never for a moment does a gentleman quit the way of Goodness. He is never so harried but that he cleaves to this; never so tottering but that he cleaves to this.

4.6

子曰："我未见好仁者，恶不仁者。好仁者，无以尚之；恶不仁者，其为仁矣，不使不仁者加乎其身。有能一日用其力于仁矣乎？我未见力不足者。盖有之矣，我未之见也。"

【中译文】

孔子说："我没见过爱好仁德的人，也没见过憎恶不仁德的人。爱好仁德的人，是无法超越的；憎恶不仁德的人，在实行仁德时，不会让不仁德的人影响自己。有谁能在一天之内用自己的力量去实行仁德的吗？我还没见过因为力量不够的。可能会有，只是我没见过。"

【注释】

1. 尚：超过，高出。
2. 盖：发语词，表示猜疑的语气。
3. 未之见：没看到过这种人或这种情形。

【英译文】

The Master (Confucius) said, 'I have never yet seen one who really cared for Goodness, nor one who really hated wickedness. One who really cared for Goodness would never let any other consideration come first. One who hated

【中译文】

孔子说："早上明白体认了真理，晚上就死去，也是值得的。"

【注释】

1 闻：听到，知道，懂得。道：此指宇宙与人生的基本道理。

【英译文】

The Master (Confucius) said, In the morning, hear the truth in the evening, die content!

4.9

子曰："士志于道[1]，而耻恶衣恶食者，未足与议也。"

【中译文】

孔子说："知识分子有志于道，而又以穿的衣服不好，吃的饭菜不好为耻辱，这种人是不值得与他谈论的。"

【注释】

1 士：读书人，知识分子。

【英译文】

The Master (Confucius) said, A Knight whose heart is set upon the truth,

论语意解

wickedness would be so constantly doing Good that wickedness would never have a chance to get at him. Has anyone ever managed to do Good with his whole might even as long as the space of a single day? I think not. Yet I have never seen anyone give up such an attempt because he had not the strength to go on. It may well have happened, but I have never seen it.

4.7

子曰："人之过也，各于其党[1]。观过，斯知仁矣[2]。"

【中译文】

孔子说："人犯错误，有着不同的类别特征。观察一个人所犯的错误，就能知道他是哪一类人了。"

【注释】

1 党：本指古代地方组织，五百家为党。引申为朋辈，意气相投的人，同类的人。
2 斯：代词。那。仁：同"人"。一说，仁德。

【英译文】

The Master (Confucius) said, man's faults depend on the class to which he belongs. If one looks out for faults it is only as a means of recognising Goodness.

4.8

子曰："朝闻道[1]，夕死可矣。"

wickedness would be so constantly doing Good that wickedness would never have a chance to get at him. Has anyone ever managed to do Good with his whole might even as the space of a single day? I think not. Yet I have never seen anyone give up such an attempt because he had not the strength to go on. It may well have happened, but I have never seen it.

4.7

子曰："人之过也，各于其党。观过，斯知仁矣。"

【中译文】

孔子说："人的错误，有着不同的类型性征。观察一个人所犯的错误，就能知道他是怎样一类人了。"

【注释】

1. 党：本指古代地方组织，五百家为党，引申为阶级，意气相投的人，同类的人。

2. 斯：代词。那。仁：同"人"。一说，不偏，仁德。

【英译文】

The Master (Confucius) said, man's faults depend on the class to which he belongs. If one looks out for faults it is only as a means of recognising Goodness.

4.8

子曰："朝闻道，夕死可矣。"

【中译文】

孔子又说："早上明白体认了真理，晚上死去也行，也是值得的。"

【注释】

1. 闻：晓得。道：懂得，道，此指宇宙万物主的基本道理。

【英译文】

The Master (Confucius) said, In the morning, hear the truth; in the evening die content!

4.9

子曰："士志于道，而耻恶衣恶食者，未足与议也。"

【中译文】

孔子说："知识分子有志于道，而又以穿的衣服不华美、吃的饭菜不够美味为耻辱，这种人是不值得与他谈论的。"

【注释】

1. 士：读书人，知识分子。

【英译文】

The Master (Confucius) said, A Knight whose heart is set upon the truth...

【英译文】

The Master (Confucius) said, A gentleman in his dealings with the world has neither enmities nor affections; but wherever he sees Right he ranges himself beside it :

4.11

子曰："君子怀德，小人怀土[1]；君子怀刑[2]，小人怀惠。"

【中译文】

孔子说："君子关注仁德教化，小人关注生计安乐；君子关注守法遵纪，小人关注实际利益。"

【注释】

1 土：乡土田宅，具体物质生活。
2 刑：指法度，典范。

【英译文】

The Master (Confucius) said, Where a gentleman sets their hearts upon moral force a petty man sets theirs upon the soil. Where a gentleman thinks only of punishments, a petty man thinks only of exemptions.

4.12

子曰："放于利而行[1]，多怨。"

论语意解

七七
六五

---

but who is ashamed of wearing shabby clothes and eating coarse food, is not worth calling into counsel.

4.10

子曰："君子之于天下也，无适也，无莫也[1]，义之与比[2]。"

【中译文】

孔子说："君子对于天下事情，既无统一标准，也不是完全没标准，而是根据具体情况作为处理标准。"

【注释】

1 适，莫：各家有三种解释：一、《集释》毛奇龄《论语稽术篇》："适"，厚也。"莫"，薄也。"无适无莫"，是一视同仁，对人用情无亲疏厚薄，不要一味亲近，一味冷淡。二、"适"，通"敌"，指敌对。"莫"通"慕"，爱慕。"无　适无莫"，是"无所为仇，无所欣慕"。三、《正义》："适（dí）"，主，专主，固定不变。"莫"，不肯，没有。"无适无莫"，是无可无不可，没有一成不变的。君子处理天下的事，没有一定要做的，也没有一定不要做的，而是唯义是从，只要合情合理就可以。

2 义之与比：与义靠近，向义靠拢，也就是"与义比"。"比（bì）"，从，靠近，亲近。

【英译文】

The Master (Confucius) said, A gentleman in his dealings with the world has neither enmities nor affections; but wherever he sees right he ranges himself beside it.

4.11

子曰："君子怀德，小人怀土；君子怀刑，小人怀惠。"

【中译文】

孔子说："君子关注的是道德教化，小人关注的是生存条件；君子关注的是法度规范，小人关注的是恩惠私利。"

【注释】

1. 怀：思念。具体所指生活。

2. 土：指乡土、田地。

【英译文】

The Master (Confucius) said, Where a gentleman sets his hearts upon moral force a petty man sets theirs upon the soil. Where a gentleman thinks only of punishments, a petty man thinks only of exemptions.

4.12

子曰："放于利而行，多怨。"

但 who is ashamed of wearing shabby clothes and eating coarse food, is not worth calling into counsel.

4.10

子曰："君子之于天下也，无适也，无莫也，义之与比。"

【中译文】

孔子说："君子对于天下事情，既无所贪慕亲近，也不是完全疏离，而是根据具体情况作为办事遵从道义。"

【注释】

1. 适、莫：各家有三种解释：一，读音为"dí"，毛奇龄《论语稽求篇》："适，敌也。莫，慕也。"意思是"无所敌对，无所贪慕。"对人用情不来疏薄厚，不要一味地……二，读"适"为"敌"，"莫"通"慕"，爱慕。"无适无莫"，是"无所为也，无所不为"。——（北大）。三，适，主。"适（dí）"，专，专主。"莫"，不肯。意为"无可无不可"，没有一成不变，君子心理天下的事，没有一定要做的，也没有一定不要做的，而是唯义是从，只要合情合理就可以。

2. 义之与比：与义靠近，向义看拢，也就是"与义比"。比（bǐ），从，靠近，亲近。

【英译文】

The Master (Confucius) said, If it is really possible to govern a state by ritual and yielding, there is no more to be said. But if it is not really possible, of what use is ritual?

4.14

子曰："不患无位，患所以立¹。不患莫己知，求为可知也。"

【中译文】

孔子说："不要担忧没有官位，应担忧的是自己本事如何；不担忧没有人知道自己，只求自己有值得别人知道的德才。"

【注释】

1 立：站得住脚，有职位，在社会有立足之地。

【英译文】

The Master (Confucius) said, A gentleman does not mind not being in office; all he minds about is whether he has qualities that entitle him to office. He does not mind failing to get recognition; he is too busy doing the things that entitle him to recognition.

4.15

子曰："参乎！吾道一以贯之。"曾子曰："唯¹。"子出，门人问曰："何谓也？"曾子曰：

【中译文】

孔子说："只依据私利而行动，会招致众多的怨恨。"

【注释】

1 放：通"仿"。仿照，效法，依照。引申为一味追求。

【英译文】

The Master (Confucius) said, Those whose measures are dictated by mere expediency will arouse continual discontent.

4.13

子曰："能以礼让为国乎¹，何有²？不能以礼让为国，如礼何？"

【中译文】

孔子说："能够以礼让治国，那还有什么困难呢？如果不能以礼让来治国，徒具礼仪之形式又有什么用呢？"

【注释】

1 礼让：按照周礼，注重礼仪与谦让。
2 何有：指有什么，这里指有什么困难呢，指不难。

【英译文】

The Master (Confucius) said, If it is really possible to govern a state by ritual and yielding, there is no more to be said. But if it is not really possible, of what use is ritual?

4.14

子曰："不患无位，患所以立；不患莫己知，求为可知也。"

【中译文】

孔子说："不要担忧没有官位，应当忧虑的是自己凭什么本事站得住脚；不担忧没人知道自己，只求自己有值得别人知道的能力。"

【注释】

1　立：站得住脚，不用指……在社会有立足之地。

【英译文】

The Master (Confucius) said, A gentleman does not mind not being in office; all he minds about is whether he has qualities that entitle him to office. He does not mind failing to get recognition; he is too busy doing the things that entitle him to recognition.

4.15

子曰："参乎！吾道一以贯之。"曾子曰："唯。"子出，门人问曰："何谓也？"曾子曰：……

【中译文】

孔子说："……只依靠礼让来行事，会怎么样的呢。"

【注释】

1　让：谦逊。引申为……犹言……引申为一……

【英译文】

The Master (Confucius) said, Those whose measures are dictated by mere expediency will arouse continual discontent.

4.13

子曰："能以礼让为国乎，何有？不能以礼让为国，如礼何？"

【中译文】

孔子说："……能够以礼让治国，那还有什么困难呢？如果不能以礼让来治国，那具体礼仪又有什么用呢？"

【注释】

1　礼让：以礼相让，谦逊礼让以讲让。
2　何有：有什么……这里指有什么困难呢，指不难。

【注释】

1 喻：明白，懂得。义：公正合宜的道理或举动，合乎正义。

2 利：私利，财利。

【英译文】

The Master (Confucius) said, A gentleman takes as much trouble to discover what is right as a pettyman takes to discover what will pay.

4.17

子曰："见贤思齐焉[1]，见不贤而内自省也[2]。"

【中译文】

孔子说："看到贤人，就想到要向他看齐，看到不贤的人，就应该两相对照自我反省。"

【注释】

1 贤：贤人，有德行有才能的人。齐：平等，向……看齐，与……同等。

2 省（xǐng）：反省，内省，检查自己的思想行为。

【英译文】

The Master (Confucius) said, In the presence of a good man, think all the time how you may learn to equal him. In the presence of a bad man, turn your gaze within!

论语意解

八○ 七九

"夫子之道忠恕而已矣[2]。"

【中译文】

孔子说："曾参啊！我的学说是有一个根本的宗旨贯彻始终。"曾子说："是。"孔子走出去以后，别的弟子问："是什么意思呢？"曾子说："老师所主张的道，不过是忠和恕罢了。"

【注释】

1 唯：在这里是应答词。是的。

2 忠：尽自己之力待他人，诚实不欺。恕：由自身反推到他人所犯的错失、设身处地地理解与宽容别人。

【英译文】

The Master (Confucius) said, Shen! My Way has one (thread) that runs right through it. Zeng Shen said, I agree. When the Master had gone out, someone asked, What did he mean? Zeng Shen said, Our Master's Way is simply this: Loyalty, consideration.

4.16

子曰："君子喻于义[1]，小人喻于利[2]。"

【中译文】

孔子说："君子懂得大义，小人懂得私利。"

论语意释

"夫子之道忠恕而已矣。"

【中译文】

孔子说："曾参啊！我的学说是有一个根本的宗旨贯彻始终。"曾子说："是。"孔子走出去以后，别的弟子问道："是什么意思呢？"曾子说："老师所主张的道，不过是忠和恕罢了。"

【注释】

1 唯：在这里是应答词，是的。

2 忠：尽自己之力待他人，做实不欺。恕：由自己推想到别人而言的话，设身处地地理解与宽容别人。

【英译文】

The Master (Confucius) said, Shen! My Way has one (thread) that runs right through it. Zeng Shen said, I agree. When the Master had gone out, some-one asked, What did he mean? Zeng Shen said, Our Master's Way is simply this: Loyalty, consideration.

4.16

子曰："君子喻于义，小人喻于利。"

【中译文】

孔子说："君子懂得大义，小人懂得私利。"

【注释】

1 喻：明白，懂得。义：公正合宜的道理或举动，合乎正义。

2 利：私利，财利。

【英译文】

The Master (Confucius) said, A gentleman takes as much trouble to discover what is right as a pettyman takes to discover what will pay.

4.17

子曰："见贤思齐焉，见不贤而内自省也。"

【中译文】

孔子说："看到贤人，就应该是向他看齐；看到不贤的人，就应该反省自己有没有和他相似的毛病。"

【注释】

1 贤：贤人，有德行有才能的人。齐：平等，向……看齐，与……同等。

2 省（xǐng）：反省，内省，检查自己的思想行为。

【英译文】

The Master (Confucius) said, In the presence of a good man, think all the time how you may learn to equal him. In the presence of a bad man, turn your gaze within!

【注 释】

1 游：离家出游。如"游学"、"游宦"。

2 游必有方：指让父母知道所游的确定地方，而不要无固定地方地随处飘泊，致使父母挂念担心。"方"，方向方位。

【英译文】

The Master (Confucius) said, While your parents are alive, do not wander far afield; if you do so, go only where you have said you were going.

4.20

子曰："三年无改于父之道，可谓孝矣[1]。"

【中译文】

孔子说："父亲死后，如果三年的行为都不改变，父道如在眼前，这样的人可以说是做到了孝。"

【注 释】

1 "三年"句：又见《学而篇第一》第十章。

【英译文】

The Master (Confucius) said, If for the whole three years of mourning a son manages to carry on the household exactly as in his father's day, then he is a good son indeed.

论语意解

4.18

子曰："事父母几谏[1]。见志不从，又敬不违，劳而不怨[2]。"

【中译文】

孔子说："侍奉父母，如果发现他们有不对的地方，要委婉地进行劝说。父母不愿听从意见，还是要恭恭敬敬，而不要违背；为父母操劳而不生怨恨。"

【注 释】

1 几（jī）：委婉，轻微，隐微。

2 劳：忧愁，忧虑。

【英译文】

The Master (Confucius) said, In serving his parents a man may gently remonstrate with them. But if he sees that he has failed to change their opinion, he should resume an attitude of deference andmt offend them; may feel discouraged, but not resentful.

4.19

子曰："父母在，不远游[1]，游必有方[2]。"

【中译文】

孔子说："父母在世，不要远离家乡；如果不得已离开家乡，也必须有一定的方位。"

4.18

子曰："事父母几谏。见志不从，又敬不违，劳而不怨。"

【中译文】

孔子说："侍奉父母，如果发现他们有不对的地方，要委婉地进行劝阻。父母不愿从自己的意见，还是要恭敬，而不要在冒犯；为父母操劳而不生怨恨。"

【注释】

1. 几(jī)：委婉，轻微，微谏。
2. 劳：忧愁，担忧。

【英译文】

The Master (Confucius) said, In serving his parents a man may gently remonstrate with them. But if he sees that he has failed to change their opinion, he should resume an attitude of deference and not offend them; may feel discouraged, but not resentful.

4.19

子曰："父母在，不远游，游必有方。"

【中译文】

孔子说："父母在世，不要远游离家；如果不得已离开家乡，也必须有一定的方位。"

【注释】

1. 游家出游：游，指学；方，常也。
2. 游必有方：指出外求知道所往的确定地方，而不要无固定地方地随处乱跑，这使父母挂念也心。"方"，方向方位。

【英译文】

The Master (Confucius) said, While your parents are alive, do not wander far afield; if you do so, go only where you have said you were going.

4.20

子曰："三年无改于父之道，可谓孝矣。"

【中译文】

孔子说："父亲死后，如果三年的行为对其不改变，父道如在眼前，这样的人才可以就是孝顺了孝。"

【注释】

1. "三年"句：又见《学而篇第一》第十一章。

【英译文】

The Master (Confucius) said, If for the whole three years of mourning a son manages to carry on the household exactly as in his father's day, then he is a good son indeed.

【注释】

1 古者：古代的人，也往往指古代有统治地位的、做官的人。

2 耻：羞愧，耻辱。在这里是意动用法，以……为耻。"行"比"言"难，"行"往往赶不上"言"；说了话，如果做不到，就会感到失信的耻辱。躬：亲身，亲自。这里指自己的行动。逮：赶上。

【英译文】

The Master (Confucius) said, In old days a man kept a hold on his words, fearing the disgrace that would ensue should he himself fail to keep pace with them.

4.23

子曰："以约失之者鲜矣[1]。"

【中译文】

孔子说："因约束自己而犯错的人是很少的。"

【注释】

1 约：约束，检束，谨慎节制。这里指以一种立身处世的原则标准经常来约束自己。失：过失，犯错误。鲜：少。

【英译文】

The Master (Confucius) said, Those who are strict with themselves rarely

4.21

子曰："父母之年，不可不知也。一则以喜，一则以惧[1]。"

【中译文】

孔子说："父母的年龄，不可以不知道。一方面为他们长寿而高兴，一方面为他们日益衰老而担心。"

【注释】

1 惧：父母年纪大了就必然日益衰老、接近死亡，故忧惧担心。

【英译文】

The Master (Confucius) said, It is always better for a man to know the age of his parents. In the one case such knowledge will be a comfort to him; in the other, it will fill him with a salutary dread.

4.22

子曰："古者言之不出[1]，耻躬之不逮也[2]。"

【中译文】

孔子说："古人不轻易把话说出来，是因为认为说出来却做不到是耻辱的。"

论语意解

论语意释

4.21

子曰:"父母之年,不可不知也。一则以喜,一则以惧。"

【中译文】

孔子说:"父母的年龄,不可以不知道。一方面为他们长寿而高兴,一方面为他们日益衰老而担心。"

【注释】

1. 惧:父母半纪大了必然日益衰老者,故惧忧也。

【英译文】

The Master (Confucius) said, It is always better for a man to know the age of his parents. In the one case such knowledge will be a comfort to him; in the other, it will fill him with a salutary dread.

4.22

子曰:"古者言之不出,耻躬之不逮也。"

【中译文】

孔子说:"古人不轻易把话说出来,是因为以做不到为可耻的。"

【注释】

1. 古者:古代的人,也指在古代有着高地位的、做官的人。
2. 耻:羞愧,耻辱。在这里意为动用法,这……为耻。躬:"行","言"反,在这排不上"言";反了后,谨慎不迎,就会感到失信的耻事。躬:亲身,这里指自己的行为。逮:赶上。

【英译文】

The Master (Confucius) said, In old days a man kept a hold on his words, fearing the disgrace that would ensue should he himself fail to keep pace with them.

4.23

子曰:"以约失之者鲜矣。"

【中译文】

孔子说:"因约束自己而犯过错的人是很少的。"

【注释】

1. 约:约束,谨慎节制。这里指以世的原则标准经常来约束自己。矣:过失,犯错。鲜:少。

【英译文】

The Master (Confucius) said, Those who are strict with themselves rarely

【注释】

1 邻：邻人，邻居。这里指思想品格一致，志向相同，能共同合作的人。

【英译文】

The Master (Confucius) said, Moral force never dwells in solitude; it will always bring neighbours.

4.26

子游曰："事君数[1]，斯辱矣[2]；朋友数，斯疏矣。"

【中译文】

子游说："侍奉君主，如果频繁地提不同意见，就会招致羞辱；对待朋友，如果频繁地提不同意见，就会遭到疏远。"

【注释】

1 数（shuò）：屡次，多次。这里指频繁、烦琐地提意见，过分地反复进行劝谏。朱子所注《论语》引用胡氏的注说："事君，谏不行，则当去；导友，善不纳，则当止。至于烦渎，则言者轻、听者厌矣。是以求荣而反辱，求亲而反疏也。"

2 斯：副词。就。

make mistakes.

4.24

子曰："君子欲讷于言[1]，而敏于行[2]。"

【中译文】

孔子说："君子说话要谨慎，而做事要勤奋敏捷。"

【注释】

1 讷：本义是说话言语迟钝。这里指说话谨慎，留有余地。

2 敏于行："行"，行动，行为。

【英译文】

The Master (Confucius) said, A gentleman should be cautious in word but prompt in deed.

4.25

子曰："德不孤，必有邻[1]。"

【中译文】

孔子说："具备仁德就不会孤立，必然会有相同品行的人成为朋友。"

论语简说

【注释】

1. 邻：邻人，邻居。这里指思想品格一致、志向相同，常共同合作的人。

【英译文】

The Master (Confucius) said, Moral force never dwells in solitude; it will always bring neighbours.

4.26

子游曰："事君数¹，斯辱矣；朋友数，斯疏矣。"

【中译文】

子游说："侍奉君主，如果频繁地提不同意见，就会招致羞辱；对待朋友，如果频繁地提不同意见，就会遭到疏远。"

【注释】

1. 数（shuò）：密，多次。这里指频繁、喋喋不休地提意见，过分地反复进行劝谏。朱子原注《论语》引用胡氏的注说："事君，谏不行，则当去；导友，善不纳，则止。至于烦渎，则言者轻，听者厌矣。是以求荣而反辱，求亲而反疏也。"

2. 斯：则，就。

4.24

子曰："君子欲讷于言¹，而敏于行²。"

【中译文】

孔子说："君子说话要谨慎，而做事要勤奋敏捷。"

【注释】

1. 讷：本义是说话迟钝或木讷，这里指谨慎而说，留有余地。

2. 敏于行："行"，行动，行为。

【英译文】

The Master (Confucius) said, A gentleman should be cautious in word but prompt in deed.

4.25

子曰："德不孤，必有邻¹。"

【中译文】

孔子说："具备仁德的人不会孤立，必然会有和他品行相同的人成为邻友。"

论语意解

【英译文】

Zi You said, In the service of one's prince repeated scolding can only lead to loss of favour; in friendship, it brings estrangement.

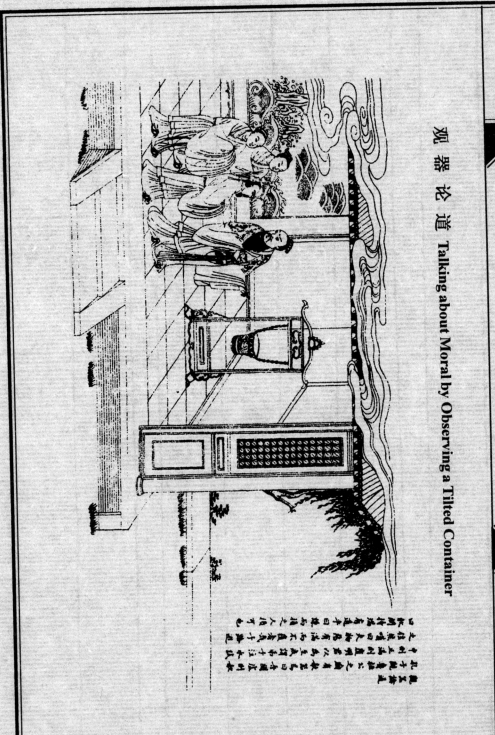

观器论道 Talking about Moral by Observing a Tilted Container

论语营绎

观器论道 Talking about Moral by Observing a Tilted Container

【英译文】

Zi You said, In the service of one's prince repeated scolding can only lead to loss of favour; in friendship, it brings estrangement.

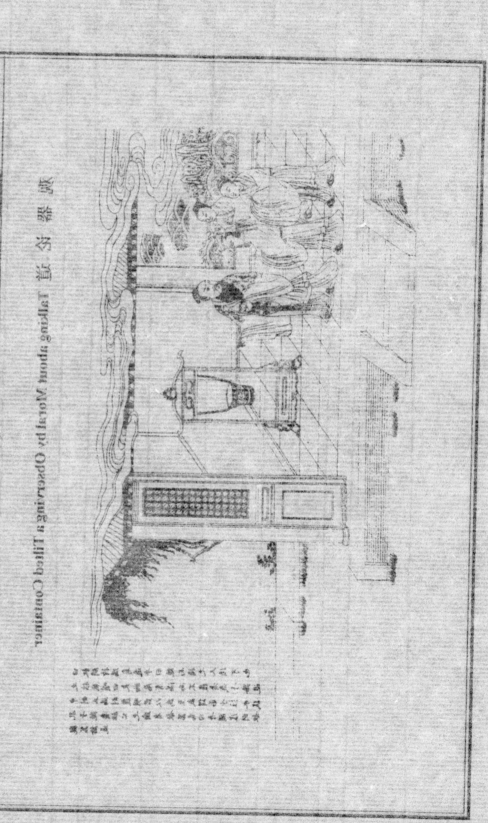

公冶长篇第五（共二十八章）

Talking about the Important People

5.1

子谓公冶长[1]："可妻也[2]。虽在缧绁之中[3]，非其罪也。"以其子妻之[4]。

【中译文】

孔子说到公冶长："可以把女儿嫁给他做妻子。他虽然被囚禁在监狱中，但不是他的罪过。"于是把女儿嫁给了公冶长。

【注释】

1 公冶长：姓公冶，名长，字子芝。鲁国人（一说，齐国人）。孔子的弟子。传说懂得鸟语。

2 妻：本是名词，在这里作动词用，读（qì）。把女儿嫁给他。

3 缧绁（léi xiè）：捆绑犯人用的黑色的长绳子。这里代指监狱。

4 子：指自己的女儿。

【英译文】

The Master (Confucius) said of Gongye Chang, Though he was once jailed, he is not an unfit person to choose as a husband; for it was not through any fault of his own, He married him to his daughter.

5.2

子谓南容[1]："邦有道[2]，不废[3]；邦无道，免于刑戮[4]。"以其兄之子妻之。

【中译文】

孔子谈论南容，说："国家治理有方的时候，他能被任用；国家无道的时候，他能免受迫害。"于是把自己的侄女嫁给了南容。

【注释】

1 南容：姓南宫，名适（kuò），一作"括"，又名绍（tāo），字子容。鲁国孟僖子之子，孟懿子之兄（一说，弟），本名仲孙阅，因居于南宫，以之为姓。谥号敬叔，故也称南宫敬叔。孔子的弟子。

2 邦有道：指社会秩序好，政治清明，局面稳定，政权巩固，国家太平兴盛。

3 废：废弃，废置不用。

4 刑戮："戮（lù）"，杀。刑戮，泛指受刑罚，受惩治，受迫害。

【英译文】

The Master (Confucius) said of Nan Rong, In a country ruled according to the way, he would not be out of office; in a country not ruled according to the Way, he would manage to avoid capital punishment or mutilation. He married him to his elder brother's daughter.

公冶长篇第五 (共二十八章)

Talking about the Important People

5.1

子谓公冶长：“可妻也。虽在缧绁之中，非其罪也。”以其子妻之。

【中译文】

孔子谈到公冶长："可以把女儿嫁给他做妻子。他虽然被因禁在牢狱中，但不是他的罪过。"于是把女儿嫁给了公冶长。

【注释】

1 公冶长：姓公冶，名长，字子长，鲁国人（一说齐国人）。孔子的弟子。他的事迹不详。
2 妻：本是名词，在这里作动词用。娶 (qī)，把女子嫁给他。
3 缧绁 (lei xie)：捆绑犯人用的黑色的长绳子。这里代指监狱。
4 子：指自己的女儿。

【英译文】

The Master (Confucius) said of Gongye Chang, Though he was once jailed, he is not an unfit person to choose as a husband, for it was not through any fault of his own. He married him to his daughter.

5.2

子谓南容："邦有道，不废；邦无道，免于刑戮。"以其兄之子妻之。

【中译文】

孔子谈论南容，说："国家治理有方的时候，他不会被弃用；国家无道的时候，他能免受追害。"于是孔子把自己的侄女嫁给了南容。

【注释】

1 南容：姓南宫，名适 (kuo)，一作"括"，又名绦 (tao)，字子容。曾因孟僖子之子，孟懿子之兄 (一说之弟)，本名仲孙阅，因居于南宫，故出称南宫縚或仲。孔子的弟子。
2 邦有道：指社会安宁，政治清明，局面稳定，政权巩固，国家太平兴盛。
3 废：废弃，搁置不用。
4 刑戮："刑"，禁；判罪。"戮 (lù)"，杀。刑戮，受刑罚或被杀。受迫害。

【英译文】

The Master Confucius (said of Nan Rong, In a country ruled according to the Way, he would not be out of office; in a country not ruled according to the Way, he would manage to avoid capital punishment or mutilation. He married him to his elder brother's daughter.

5.4

子贡问曰："赐也何如[1]？"子曰："女[2]，器也。"曰："何器也？"曰："瑚琏也[3]。"

【中译文】

子贡问孔子："你认为我怎么样呢？"孔子说："你是个有用的器具。"子贡问："是个什么器具呢？"孔子说："是敬神的玉器。"

【注释】

1 何如：如何，怎样。

2 女：汝，你。

3 瑚琏：古代祭祀时盛粮食（黍稷）用的一种贵重的器具，竹制，上面用玉装饰，很华美，有方形的，有圆形的，夏代称"瑚"，殷代称"琏"。在这里，孔子用"瑚琏"比喻子贡是有用之材，但相比"君子不器"而言，有所差距。

【英译文】

Zi Gong asked, What do you think of me? The Master said, You are a vessel. Zi Gong said, What sort of vessel? The Master said, A fine sacrificial vessel.

5.5

或曰[1]："雍也仁而不佞[2]。"子曰："焉用

5.3

子谓子贱[1]："君子哉若人[2]！鲁无君子者，斯焉取斯[3]？"

【中译文】

孔子谈论子贱，说："真是君子啊这个人！假如说鲁国没有君子，他从何处获得这种品德呢？"

【注释】

1 子贱：姓宓（fú），名不齐，字子贱，鲁国人。公元前521年生，卒年不详。孔子的弟子。比孔子小四十九岁。子贱曾任单父（今山东省单县）宰，史称："有才智，爱百姓，身不下堂，鸣琴而治。能尊师取友，以成其德。"著有《宓子》十六篇。

2 若：代词。此，这。

3 斯：代词。在句中，第一个"斯"，是代指子贱这个人。第二个"斯"，是代指君子的品德。焉：疑问代词。哪里，怎么，怎样。取：取得，获得。

【英译文】

Of Zi Jian the Master said, A gentleman indeed is such a one as he! If the land of Lu state were indeed without gentlemen, how could he have learnt this?

论语意解

5.4

子贡问曰："赐也何如？"子曰："女，器也。"曰："何器也？"曰："瑚琏也。"

【中译文】

子贡问孔子："你看我怎么样呢？"孔子说："你是个有用的器具。"子贡问："是个什么器具呢？"孔子说："是盛黍稷的玉器。"

【注释】

1 何如：怎样，怎么样。
2 女：汝，你。
3 瑚琏：古代祭祀时盛粮食（黍稷）用的一种贵重的器具，竹制成，上面用玉装饰，很华美，特别尊贵的。夏代叫"瑚"，殷代叫"琏"。在这里，孔子用"瑚琏"比喻子贡是有用之材，由相比："君子不器"，而言，有所差别。

【英译文】

Zi Gong asked, What do you think of me? The Master said, You are a vessel. Zi Gong said, What sort of vessel? The Master said, A fine sacrificial vessel.

5.5

或曰："雍也仁而不佞。"子曰："焉用

5.3

子谓子贱："君子哉若人！鲁无君子者，斯焉取斯？"

【中译文】

孔子谈论子贱，说："真是个君子啊这个人！假如鲁国没有君子，他从何处获得这种品德呢？"

【注释】

1 子贱：姓宓（伏），名不齐，字子贱，鲁国人。公元前521年生，卒年不详。孔子的弟子，比孔子小四十九岁。一度曾任单父（今山东省单县）宰，史称："有才智，爱百姓，身不下堂，鸣琴而治，很受爱戴。以彰其德。"著有《宓子》十六篇。
2 若：代词，此，这。
3 斯：代词。句初中，第一个"斯"，是代指君子这个人。第二个"斯"，是代指君子的品德。焉：疑问代词，哪里，怎么。取：取得，获得。

【英译文】

Of Zi Jian the Master said, A gentleman indeed is such a one as he! If the land of a state were indeed without gentlemen, how could he have learnt this?

子说³。

【中译文】

孔子让漆雕开去做官，漆雕开回答："我对做官还没有信心。"孔子很高兴。

【注释】

1 漆雕开：姓漆雕，名开，字子开（一说，字子若）。蔡国人（一说，鲁国人）。公元前540年生，卒年不详。孔子弟子。

2 "吾斯"句："吾未能信斯"的倒装。"斯"做官的事。"信"，信心，相信，自信。

3 说：同"悦"。

【英译文】

The Master (Confucius) gave Qidiao Kai leave to take office, but he replied, 'I have not yet sufficiently perfected myself in the virtue of good faith.' The Master was pleased.

5.7

子曰："道不行，乘桴浮于海¹。从我者²，其由与³！"子路闻之喜。子曰："由也好勇过我，无所取材⁴。"

【中译文】

孔子说："我的主张得不到实行，就乘木筏到海上

论语意解

九四　九三

佞？御人以口给³，屡憎于人，不知其仁，焉用佞？"

【中译文】

有的人说："冉雍有仁德，却不能言善辩。"孔子说："何必要能言善辩呢？同人家巧言善辩，常常引起别人的厌恶。我不知道冉雍是否有仁德，但何必能巧言善辩呢？"

【注释】

1 或：代词。有的人。

2 雍：姓冉，名雍，字仲弓。鲁国人。生于公元前522年，卒年不详。孔子的弟子。佞（nìng）：强嘴利舌，花言巧语。

3 御：抗拒，抵抗。这里指辩驳对方，与人争论。口给："给（jǐ）"，本义是丰足，也指言语敏捷。口给，指嘴巧，嘴快话多。孔子反对"巧言乱德"的人。

【英译文】

Someone said, Ran Yong is Good, but he is a poor talker. The Master said, What need has he to be a good talker? Those who down others with clap-trap are seldom popular. Whether he is Good, I do not know. But I see no need for him to be a good talker.

5.6

子使漆雕开仕¹，对曰："吾斯之未能信²。"

论语意读

5.6

【中译文】

有的人说："冉雍有仁德，却不能言善辩。"孔子说："何必要能言善辩呢？同人家巧言善辩，常常被人讨厌。冉雍有没有仁德，我不知道，但何必要能言善辩呢？"

【注释】

1. 佞：伶俐。有口才。
2. 雍：冉雍，字仲弓，鲁国人，生于公元前522年，少孔子二十九岁，孔子的弟子。樗(níng)：温顺和善，花言巧语。
3. 御：抵挡，抵抗。这里指善辩地对答，与人争论。口给："给(jǐ)"，本义是丰足，由指言辞敏捷。口论，能说会道，嘴快话多。孔子反对"巧言乱德"。故人……

【英译文】

Someone said, Ran Yong is Good, but he is a poor talker. The Master said, What need has he to be a good talker? Those who do down others with clap-trap are seldom popular. Whether he is Good, I do not know. But I see no need for him to be a good talker.

5.7

子曰："道不行，乘桴浮于海。从我者，其由与？"子路闻之喜。子曰："由也好勇过我，无所取材。"

【中译文】

孔子说："我的主张得不到实行，便乘木筏到海上……

子使漆雕开仕。对曰："吾斯之未能信。"子说。

【中译文】

孔子让漆雕开去做官。漆雕开回答说："我对做官这事还没有信心。"孔子很高兴。

【注释】

1. 漆雕开：姓漆雕，名开，字子开（一说，字子若）。蔡国人（一说，鲁国人）。公元前540年生，少孔本者，孔子弟子。
2. 斯：此，指"君不能信道"的治国事。信：信心，自信。
3. 说：同"悦"。

【英译文】

The Master (Confucius) gave Qidiao Kai leave to take office, but he replied, 'I have not yet sufficiently perfected myself in the virtue of good faith.' The Master was pleased.

之宰也⁴，不知其仁也。""赤也何如⁵？" 子曰："赤也，束带立于朝⁶，可使与宾客言也，不知其仁也。"

【中译文】

孟武伯问："子路能达到仁吗？"孔子又说："不知道。"他又问。孔子说："仲由啊，在一个有千辆兵车的国家里，可以让他管理赋税，掌握军政，但是我不知道他能不能达到仁。"孟武伯问："冉求怎么样？"孔子说："冉求啊，可以让他在一个有千户人家的地方，或在有百辆兵车的部族里，担任总管。但是我不知道他能不能达到仁。"孟武伯问："公西赤怎么样？"孔子说："公西赤啊，可以让他穿上礼服，系上袍带，站在朝廷大堂上，接待宾客，但是我也不知道他能不能达到仁。"

【注释】

1 治其赋：古代以田赋地税出兵役，故称兵为赋。治其赋，含有负责管理军事政治的意思。

2 邑：古代居民的聚居点，相当于后世的城镇，周围的土地也归属于邑。邑，又可以分为"公邑"，"采邑"。"公邑"，是直辖于诸侯的领地属地；"采邑"是由诸侯分封给所属的卿、大夫的领地。文中"千室之邑"，指的是居有一千户人家的城邑，当指"公邑"。

论语意解

九六

九五

漂流去。能跟随我的人，大概只有仲由吧！"子路听了这话很高兴。孔子接着说："仲由啊，争强好勇超过了我，就是不会裁度事理，自我把握。"

【注释】

1 桴（fú）：用竹或木编成当船用的水上交通工具，大的叫"筏"，小一点的叫"桴"。

2 从：跟从，跟随。

3 其：语助词，表示揣测。大概，可能。与：同"欤"。语助词，表疑问，与"乎"同。

4 材：同"哉"。语助词。一说，同"才"。才能。另说，同"裁"。裁度事理。

【英译文】

The Master (Confucius) said, The Way makes no progress. I shall get upon a raft and float out to sea. I am sure Zhong You would come with me. Zi Lu on hearing of this was delighted. The Master said, That is Zhong You indeed! He sets far too much store by feats of physical daring. It seems as though I should never get hold of the right sort of people.

5.8

孟武伯问："子路仁乎？"子曰："不知也。"又问，子曰："由也，千乘之国，可使治其赋也¹，不知其仁也。""求也何如？"子曰："求也，千室之邑²，百乘之家³，可使为

【英译文】

The Master (Confucius) said, The Way makes no progress. I shall get upon a raft and put out to sea. I am sure Zhong You would come with me! Zhong You is fonder of daring than I, but he does not know how to go about things.

On hearing this the Master said, That You was braver than I. He sets far too much store by deeds of physical daring. It seems as though there were no way of getting at the right sort of people to...

【中译文】

孔子问子贡："你与颜回相比，谁更厉害？"子贡回答："我怎么敢同颜回比呢？颜回听到一件事可以推知十件事，我听到一件事只能推知两件事。"孔子说："确实比不上他，我与你都比不上他。"

【注释】

1 女：汝，你。
2 孰：谁。愈：胜过，更好，更强，更厉害。
3 望：比。
4 弗：不。
5 与：动词。赞同，同意。

【英译文】

The Master (Confucius) said to Zi Gong, Which do you yourself think is the better, you or Yan Hui? He answered, I dare not so much as look at Yan Hui. For Yan Hui has but to hear one part in ten, in order to understand the whole ten. Whereas if I hear one part, I understand no more than two parts. The Master said, Not equal to him-you and I are not equal to him!

5.10

宰予昼寝。子曰："朽木不可雕也，粪土之墙不可杇也[1]。于予与何诛[2]？"子曰："始吾于人也，听其言而信其行；今吾于人也，听其言而观其行。于予与改是[3]。"

---

3 家：指的是卿、大夫的采地食邑。家可设"家臣"，以管理政务。
4 宰：最早的意思是奴隶的总管。后来是官吏的通称。邑的行政长官也称宰（相当于县长）。
5 赤：姓公西，名赤，字子华，鲁国人。公元前509年生，卒年不详。孔子的弟子。
6 束带：整理衣服，扎好衣带。这里指穿上礼服去上朝。

【英译文】

Meng Wubo asked whether Zi Lu was Good. The Master said, I do not know. On his repeating the question the Master said, In a country of a thousand war-chariots Zhong You could be trusted to carry out the recruiting. But whether he is Good I do not know. 'What about Qiu?' The Master said, In a city of a thousand families or a baronial family with a hundred chariots he might do well as Warden. But whether he is Good, I do not know. 'What about Gong Xichi?' The Master said, Girt with his sash, standing in his place at Court he might well be charged to converse with strangers and guests. But whether he is Good, I do not know.

5.9

子谓子贡曰："女与回也[1]，孰愈[2]？"对曰："赐也何敢望回[3]？回也闻一以知十，赐也闻一以知二。"子曰："弗如也[4]，吾与女，弗如也[5]。"

论语意解

5.8

Meng Wu Bo asked whether Zi Lu was Good. The Master said, I do not know. On his repeating the question the Master said, In a country of a thousand war-chariots Zi Lu could be trusted to carry out the recruiting. But whether he is Good I do not know.

What about Qiu? The Master said, In a city of a thousand families or a baronial family with a hundred chariots Qiu could be put in charge of the levies. But whether he is Good, I do not know.

What about Chi? The Master said, Chi, in his sash and well girt, standing in his place at Court could well be employed to converse with strangers and guests. But whether he is Good, I do not know.

【文法】

【注释】

【今译】

5.9

The Master (Confucius) said to Zi Gong, Which do you yourself think is the better, you or Hui? Zi Gong answered, How dare I so much as look at Hui? For Hui has but to hear one part in ten, in order to understand the whole ten parts, whereas if I hear one part, I understand no more than two parts.

The Master said, Not equal to him — you and I are both not equal to him.

【文法】

1 女: 汝。

2 愈: 较佳。胜过。

3 回: 颜回。

4 赐: 子贡。

5 闻一: 闻一。知十: 知十。

【注释】

【今译】

5.10

曰："枨也欲²，焉得刚？"

【中译文】

孔子说："我没见过刚毅的人。"有人回答："申枨就是。"孔子说："申枨欲望太多，怎么能算刚毅？"

【注释】

1 申枨(chéng)：姓申，名枨，字周，鲁国人。孔子的弟子。一说，就是申党(见《史记·仲尼弟子列传》)。另作"申棠"。
2 欲：欲望多。

【英译文】

The Master (Confucius) said, I have never yet seen a man who was truly steadfast. Someone answered Shen Cheng. The Master said, Shen Cheng! He is at the mercy of his desires. How can he be called steadfast?

5.12

子贡曰："我不欲人之加诸我也¹，吾亦欲无加诸人。"子曰："赐也，非尔所及也²。"

【中译文】

子贡说："我不愿别人强加于我，我也愿意不强加于人。"孔子说："子贡呀，这不是你所能做到的。"

论语意解

【中译文】

宰予白天睡大觉。孔子说："正如腐朽的木头没法再雕刻什么了，粪土的墙壁不能再粉刷了。对于宰予这个人，我没法再责备了？"孔子又说："以往，我对人，是听了他的话便相信他的行为；现在，我对人，是听了他的话还要观察他的行为。宰予这个人使我对考察人的言行有所改变。"

【注释】

1 圬(wū)：同"杇"。本指用灰泥抹墙的工具，俗称"抹子"。这里作动词用，指粉刷墙壁。
2 与：同"欤"。语气词，在这里表停顿。诛：谴责，责备，指责。
3 是：代词。此，这。在这里指代观察人的方法。

【英译文】

Zai Yu used to sleep during the day. The Master said, Rotten wood cannot be carved, nor can a wall of dried dung be trowelled. What use is there in my scolding him any more? The Master said, There was a time when I merely listened attentively to what people said, and took for granted that they would carry out their words. Now I am obliged not only to give ear to what they say, but also to keep an eye on what they do. It was my dealings with Zai Yu that brought about the change.

5.11

子曰："吾未见刚者。"或对曰："申枨¹。"子曰："枨也欲，焉得刚？"

【中译文】

孔子说："我没有见过刚毅的人。"有人回答："申枨。"孔子说："申枨欲望太多，怎么能算刚毅？"

【注释】

1 申枨(chéng)：姓申，名枨，字周，鲁国人，孔子的弟子。一说，即申党（见《史记·仲尼弟子列传》），别作"申棠"。

2 欲：贪望太多。

【英译文】

The Master (Confucius) said, I have never yet seen a man who was truly steadfast. Someone answered Shen Cheng. The Master said, Shen Cheng! He is at the mercy of his desires. How can he be called steadfast?

5.12

子贡曰："我不欲人之加诸我也，吾亦欲无加诸人。"子曰："赐也，非尔所及也。"

【中译文】

子贡说："我不愿别人强加于我，我也愿意不强加于人。"孔子说："子贡呀，这不是你所能做到的。"

【中译文】

宰予白天睡大觉。孔子说："腐朽的木头不能雕刻，用脏土筑的墙壁不能再粉刷了。对于宰予这个人，我没法责备他了？"孔子又说："以前，我对人，是听了他的话便相信他的行为；现在，我对人，听了他的话还要观察他的行为。宰予这个人使我改变了观察人的言行的态度。"

【注释】

1 杇(wū)：同"圬"，本指用来涂抹墙的工具，俗称"抹子"：这里作动词用，指粉刷墙壁。

2 诛：同"责"，责备。在这里有停顿。诛：责，责备，指责。

3 是：代词，此，这，在这里指代观察人的办法。

【英译文】

Zai Yu used to sleep during the day. The Master said, Rotten wood cannot be carved, nor can a wall of dried dung be trowelled. What use is there in my scolding him any more? The Master said, There was a time when I merely listened attentively to what people said, and took for granted that they would carry out their words. Now I am obliged not only to give ear to what they say, but also to keep an eye on what they do. It was my dealings with Zai Yu that brought about the change.

5.11

子曰："吾未见刚者。"或对曰："申枨。"子

【注释】

1 诸："之于"的合音。

2 尔：你。程子将此句与"己所不欲，勿施于人"联系起来，认为此句是"仁"，而后者是"恕"。"仁"是自然而然的，而"恕"则有所强制。

【英译文】

Zi Gong said, What I do not want others to do to me, I have no desire to do to others. The Master said, Oh! You have not quite got to that point yet.

5.13

子贡曰："夫子之文章[1]，可得而闻也；夫子之言性与天道[2]，不可得而闻也。"

【中译文】

子贡说："老师关于诗书礼乐、古代文献方面的学问，我们可以学到听到；老师关于人性和天道的论述，我们却学不到听不到。"

【注释】

1 文章：指礼乐法度、诗、书、史等各种古代文献中和的学问。

2 性：人的自然本性。天道：自然运行之道。

【英译文】

Zi Gong said, Our Master's views concerning culture and the outward insignia of goodness, we are permitted to hear, but about Man's nature and the ways of Heaven he will not tell us anything at all.

5.14

子路有闻，未之能行，唯恐有闻[1]。

【中译文】

子路听到某一道理，在还没实行的时候，唯恐又听到新的道理。

【注释】

1 有：同"又"。此处指子路闻善必行，唯恐落后。

【英译文】

When Zi Lu heard any precept and failed to put it into practice, his one fear was that he might hear some fresh precept.

5.15

子贡问曰："孔文子何以谓之'文'也[1]？"子曰："敏而好学，不耻下问，是以谓之'文'也。"

【中译文】

子贡问道："孔文子为什么谥号称作'文'呢？"孔子说："他聪敏而爱好学习，愿向下面的人请教而不以为耻，所以称他为'文'。"

【注释】

1 孔文子：卫国的执政上卿，姓孔，名圉（yǔ），字仲叔。"文"，是谥号。古代，帝王、贵族、大臣等死后，根据他生前的品德、事迹，所给予的表示褒贬的称号称谥号。"子"，是对孔圉的尊称。孔圉死于鲁哀公十五年（公元前480年）。

【英译文】

Zi Gong asked, Why was Kong Weizi called Wen (The Cultured)? The Master said, Because he was diligent and fond of learning, he was not ashamed to pick up knowledge even from his inferiors.

5.16

子谓子产[1]："有君子之道四焉：其行己也恭，其事上也敬，其养民也惠，其使民也义。"

【中译文】

孔子评价子产："他具有君子的四种德行：在行为方面，他自己很庄重，谦逊谨慎；事奉君主，他很恭敬顺从；对待老百姓，他注意给予恩惠利益；役使老百姓，他注意公平合理。"

【注释】

1 子产：名侨，字子产，郑国大夫，是郑穆公的孙子，公子发之子，担任过正卿（相当于宰相）。生年不详，卒于公元前522年。是春秋末期杰出政治家。他在郑简公、郑定公时，执政二十二年，有过许多改革措施，因而得到人民的拥护。当时曾被孔子称为"仁人"，"惠人"。

【英译文】

Of Zi Chan the Master said that in him were to be found four of the virtues that belong to the Way of the true gentleman. In his private conduct he was courteous, in serving his master he was punctilious, in providing for the needs of the people he gave them even more than their due; in exacting service from the people, he was just and reasonable.

5.17

子曰："晏平仲善与人交[1]，久而敬之[2]。"

【中译文】

孔子说："晏平仲善于同别人交往，交往时间能长且能相互敬重。"

【注释】

1 晏平仲：姓晏，名婴，字仲。夷维（今山东省高密县）人。齐国大夫，历任灵公、庄公、景公三世，

5.15

【中译文】

子贡问道："孔文子为什么谥号称作'文'呢？"孔子说："他勤敏而爱好学习，遇向下面的人请教而不以为耻，所以称他为'文'。"

【注释】

1 孔文子：卫国的执政上卿，姓孔，谥孔，名圉(yǔ)，字仲叔。"文"，是谥号。古代，帝王，贵族，大臣等死后，根据他生前的品德，事迹，朝廷予以褒贬的表示爱憎的称号，叫谥号。"子"，是对孔圉的尊称。孔圉死于鲁哀公十五年(公元前480年)。

【英译文】

Zi Gong asked, Why was Kong Weizi called Wen (The Cultured)? The Master said, Because he was diligent and fond of learning, he was not ashamed to pick up knowledge even from his inferiors.

5.16

子谓子产[1]："有君子之道四焉：其行己也恭，其事上也敬，其养民也惠，其使民也义。"

【中译文】

孔子评价子产："他具有君子的四种品德行为：本行为为恭，他自己操持重，谦逊谨慎；事奉君主，他态度恭敬；他施恩给人民，使百姓都受益处；他役使百姓，他造意必合乎理。"

【注释】

1 子产：名桥，字子产，郑国大夫，是郑穆公的孙子。公子发之子，世代正卿（相当于宰相），主车不亲，卒于公元前522年，是春秋末期杰出政治家。他在郑简公，郑定公时，执政二十二年，有过许多改革措施，因而得到人民的拥护。当时曾被孔子称为"仁人"，"惠人"。

【英译文】

Of Zi Chan the Master said that in him were to be found four of the virtues that belong to the Way of the true gentleman. In his private conduct he was courteous, in serving his master he was punctilious, in providing for the needs of the people he gave them even more than their due; in exacting service from the people, he was just and reasonable.

5.17

子曰："晏平仲善与人交[1]，久而敬之。"

【中译文】

孔子说："晏平仲善于同别人交往，交往时间越长久且能相互敬重。"

【注释】

1 晏平仲：莱县（今山东省高密县）人。齐国大夫，即传说景公，庄公，景公三世...名婴，字仲。谥平。

春秋时的蔡国，在今河南省上蔡、新蔡一带。蔡国出产大乌龟。据《淮南子·说山训》："大蔡神龟，出于沟壑。"这里用"蔡"代指大乌龟。"居"，居处，房子。这里用作动词。古代常用乌龟壳来占卜吉凶，"居蔡"指为大乌龟盖上房子藏起来以备占卜用。

2 山节藻棁："节"，是房柱子头上的斗拱；"山节"是指把斗拱雕刻成山的形状。"藻"，是水草；"棁（zhuó）"，是指房子大梁上的短柱；"藻棁"，是把短柱上画上花草图案。山节藻棁，也就是俗说的"雕梁画栋"，是古代建筑物的豪华装饰。只有天子才能把大乌龟壳藏在如此豪华的房屋里。臧文仲也这样做，显然是"越礼"行为。

3 何如：如何，怎么。知：同"智"。明智，懂事。

【英译文】

The Master (Confucius) said, Zang Wenzhong kept a Cai tortoise in a hall with the hill-pattern on its king-posts. Of what sort, pray, was his knowledge?

5.19

子张问曰："令尹子文三仕为令尹[1]，无喜色；三已之[2]，无愠色。旧令尹之政，必以告新令尹。何如？"子曰："忠矣。"曰："仁矣乎？"曰："未知。焉得仁？""崔子弑齐君[3]，陈文子有马十乘[4]，弃而违之[5]，至于他邦，则曰：'犹

曾任宰相，是当时著名政治家。生年不详，卒于公元前500年。死后，谥号为"平"，故称他"晏平仲"。传世有《晏子春秋》，系战国时人收集晏婴的言行编辑而成。善：在某一方面具有特长，擅长，长于。之：代词，代晏婴。一说，"之"指代朋友。此句意思是：晏婴与友处久，仍敬友如新。

【英译文】

The Master (Confucius) said, Yan Pingzhong is a good example of what one's intercourse with one's fellow men should be. However long he has known anyone he always maintains the same scrupulous courtesy.

5.18

子曰："臧文仲居蔡[1]，山节藻棁[2]，何如其知也[3]？"

【中译文】

孔子说："臧文仲私养了一只占卜的大龟神，把龟房的斗拱雕成山形，房梁短柱上画了水草，这个人怎么能说是聪明呢？"

【注释】

1 臧文仲：鲁国的大夫，姓臧孙，名辰，字仲。生年不详，卒于公元前617年。死后谥号"文"。曾被孔子批评为"不仁""不智"。居蔡："蔡"，

【今译】

孔子说："臧文仲给一只大乌龟盖了一间房子，房子斗栱雕成山的形状，梁上短柱画着水藻，他这个人怎么能算聪明呢？"

【英译】

The Master (Confucius) said, Ts'ang Wen-chung kept a large tortoise in a hall, with the pillar-heads ...

5.18

子张问曰："令尹子文三仕为令尹，无喜色；三已之，无愠色。旧令尹之政，必以告新令尹。何如？"

子曰："忠矣。"

曰："仁矣乎？"

曰："未知，焉得仁？"

【英译】

The Master (Confucius) said ...

5.19

"崔子弑齐君，陈文子有马十乘，弃而违之。至于他邦，则曰：'犹吾大夫崔子也。'违之。之一邦，则又曰：'犹吾大夫崔子也。'违之。何如？"

子曰："清矣。"

曰："仁矣乎？"

曰："未知，焉得仁？"

【英译】

The Master (Confucius) said ...

毕。这里指罢免，去职。

3 崔子：指齐国大夫崔杼（zhù）。他把齐庄公杀了。弑（shì）：古时称臣杀死君主或子女杀死父母。齐君：指齐庄公。姓姜，名光。

4 陈文子：齐国的大夫，名须无。崔杼杀死齐庄公时，陈文子离开齐国，两年后又返回。

5 违：离别，离开。

【英译文】

Zi chang asked, The Grand Minister Zi Wen was appointed to this office on three separate occasions, but did not on any of these three occasions display the least sign of elation. Three times he was deposed; but never showed the least sign of disappointment. Each time, he duly informed his successor concerning the administration of State affairs during his tenure of office. What should you say of him? The Master said, He was certainly faithful to his prince's interests. Zi-chang said, Would you not call him Good? The Master said, I am not sure. I see nothing in that to merit the title Good.

Zi chang said, When Cui Zi assassinated the sovereign of Qi state Chen Wenzi who held a fief of ten war chariots gave it up and went away. On arriving in another State, he said, 'I can see they are no better here than our minister Cui Zi'; and he went away. On arriving in the next country, he said, 'I can see they are no better here than our minister Cui Zi'; and went away. What should you say of him? The Master said, He was certainly scrupulous. Would you not call him Good? The Master said, I am not sure. I see nothing in that to merit the title Good.

5.20

论语意解

一〇八　一〇七

吾大夫崔子也。' 违之。之一邦，则又曰：'犹吾大夫崔子也。' 违之。何如？" 子曰："清矣。" 曰："仁矣乎？" 曰："未知。焉得仁？"

【中译文】

子张问孔子："令尹子文几次担任令尹，没表现出高兴的容色；几次被罢免，也没表现出怨恨的容色。每次免职时一定把自己旧日的一切政令公务告诉下任。这个人怎么样呢？" 孔子说："够忠诚了。" 子张说："够得上仁了吗？" 孔子说："不知道。这怎么能算是仁呢？" 子张又问："崔子杀了齐庄公，陈文子是有十驾马车的人物，舍弃不要，离开齐国。到了另一国，说：'这里的执政者好比我们的大夫崔子一样。' 又离开了。再到另一国，又说：'这里的执政者好比我们的大夫崔子一样。' 又离开了。这个人怎样呢？" 孔子说："够得上清白了。" 子张说："够得上仁了吗？" 孔子说："不知道。这怎么能算是仁呢？"

【注释】

1 令尹：楚国的官职名，相当于宰相。子文：姓鬬（dòu），名榖於菟（gòu wū tú），字子文，是楚国著名的贤相。三仕："三"是虚数，不一定只指三次，而是代表多次，几次。"仕"，是做官，担任职务。

2 三已：多次被免职。"已"，本义是停止，完，

为政篇

3 语译：楚国令尹子文三次做令尹的官，没有喜色；三次被罢免，也没有怨色。每次罢免，一定把自己做令尹时的政事全部告诉接任的人。怎么样？孔子说："忠啊。"

4 陈文子：齐国的大夫，名须无。崔杼杀齐君后，陈文子不愿事乱臣，弃其马十乘而去国，而志行信义之高洁。

5 违：离去，避开。

【英译文】

Zi chang asked, The Grand Minister Zi Wen was appointed to this office on three separate occasions, but did not on any of these three occasions display the least sign of elation. Three times he was deposed, but never showed the least sign of disappointment. Each time, he duly informed his successor concerning the administration of State affairs during his tenure of office. What should you say of him? The Master said, He was certainly faithful to his prince's interests. Zi-chang said, Would you not call him Good? The Master said, I am not sure. I see nothing in that to merit the title Good.

Zi chang said, When Cui Zi assassinated the sovereign of Qi state Chen Wen, who held a fief of ten war chariots gave it up and went away. On arriving in another State, he said, I can see they are no better here than our minister Cui Zi, and he went away. On arriving in the next country, he said, I can see they are no better here than our minister Cui Zi; and went away. What should you say of him? The Master said, He was certainly scrupulous. Would you not call him Good? I see nothing in that to merit the title Good.

【中译文】

子张问孔子："令尹子文几次担任令尹的官，没有显出高兴的容色；几次被罢免，也没有显出怨恨的容色。每次免职一定把自己任内的一切政令全部告诉接任的人。这个人怎么样呢？"孔子道："算得忠了。"子张道："算得仁吗？"孔子道："不晓得，这怎么能算是仁呢？"

"崔子杀了齐国的君主，陈文子有四十匹马，都抛弃不要，离开了齐国。到了别一国，又说：'这里的执政者同我们的大夫崔子一样，'又离开了。再到一国，又说：'这里的执政者同我们的大夫崔子一样，'又离开了。这个人怎么样呢？"孔子道："算得清白了。"子张道："算得仁吗？"孔子道："不晓得，这怎么能算是仁呢？"

【注释】

1 令尹：楚国的官名，相当于宰相。子文，姓斗（dòu），名榖於菟（gòu wū tú），字子文，是楚国著名的贤相。

2 三已：多次被免职。已，罢免，停止。

季文子三思而后行[1]。子闻之，曰："再[2]，斯可矣。"

【中译文】

季文子做某一件事往往考虑三次才行动，孔子听到这事，说："考虑两次就行了。"

【注释】

1 季文子：鲁国的大夫，姓季孙，名行父。"文"是他死后的谥号。生年不详，卒于公元前568年。历仕鲁文公、鲁宣公，至鲁成公、鲁襄公时担任正卿。

2 再：再次，第二次。作副词用，后面省略了动词"思"。此处孔子主张临事果决、过份深思熟虑、反而会夹杂私意。

【英译文】

Ji Wenzi used to think several times before acting. The Master hearing of it said, Twice quite is enough.

5.21

子曰："宁武子[1]，邦有道，则知[2]；邦无道，则愚[3]。其知可及也，其愚不可及也。"

【中译文】

孔子说："宁武子这个人当国家有道的时候，他表现得聪明；当国家无道的时候，他就表现得愚笨。他的那种聪明，别人是可以赶得上的；他的那种愚笨，别人是很难做到的。"

【注释】

1 宁武子：卫国人，庄公之子，文公、成公时的大夫。姓宁，名俞。"武"，是他死后的谥号。

2 知：同"智"。聪明，智慧。

3 愚：本义是愚笨。这里指装傻。

【英译文】

The Master (Confucius) said, Ning Wuzi 'so long as the Way prevailed in his country he showed wisdom; but when the Way no longer prevailed, he showed his folly.' To such wisdom as his we may all attain; but not to such folly!

5.22

子在陈曰[1]："归与[2]！归与！吾党之小子狂简[3]，斐然成章[4]，不知所以裁之[5]。"

【中译文】

孔子在陈国时，说："回去吧！回去吧！我们家乡的学生们，志向远大而行为粗放，且都文采斐然，我不知道该怎样去指导他们。"

【注释】

1 宁武子：卫国人，姓宁名俞，武是他的谥号。

2 知：同"智"。愚：装傻，假愚蠢。

3 愚：本义是愚蠢，这里指装傻。

【英译文】

The Master (Confucius) said, Ning Wuzi, so long as the Way prevailed in his country, showed wisdom; but when the Way no longer prevailed, he showed his folly. To such wisdom as his we may all attain but not to such folly!

5.22

子在陈曰：“归与！归与！吾党之小子狂简，斐然成章，不知所以裁之[4]。”

【中译文】

孔子在陈国时，说：“回去吧！回去吧！我们家乡的那些学生们，志向远大而行为粗疏，且都文采斐然，我不知道该怎样去裁剪他们啊。”

季文子三思而后行[1]。子闻之，曰：“再，斯可矣。”

【中译文】

季文子做某一件事都要考虑多次才去行动。孔子听说后，说：“考虑两次就可以行动了。”

【注释】

1 季文子：鲁国的大夫，姓季孙，名行父，谥号“文”。是他死后的谥号。据考证，此章不确，季文子卒于公元前568年。因而这里文公、鲁宣公、宣公成公、鲁襄公等都不可确。

2 再：两次。斯：此。此即可也。

【英译文】

Ji Wenzi used to think several times before acting. The Master, hearing of it, said, 'Twice quite is enough'

5.21

子曰：“宁武子，邦有道则知，邦无道则愚。其知可及也，其愚不可及也。”

【中译文】

孔子说：“宁武子这个人当国家政治清明时，他表现得很聪明；当国家无道的时候，他便表现得很愚笨。他的那种聪明别人可以赶得上，他的那种愚笨别人便赶不上了。”

【中译文】

　　孔子说："伯夷、叔齐不记过去的仇怨，别人对他们怨恨因此就少了。"

【注释】

1　伯夷、叔齐：是殷朝末年一个小国的国君孤竹君的两个儿子，姓墨胎。兄伯夷（一说，名允，字公信，"夷"是谥号），弟叔齐（一说，名智，字公达，"齐"是谥号）。孤竹君死后，伯夷、叔齐兄弟二人互相让位，谁都不肯做国君。后来，二人都逃到周文王所管辖的区域。周武王兴兵伐纣时，他们曾拦车马进行劝阻。周灭殷后，传说他们二人对改朝换代不满而耻食周粟，隐居在首阳山，采薇（一种野菜）为食，终于饿死。

2　是用：因此。希：同"稀"。少。

【英译文】

The Master said, Bo Yi and Shu Qi never bore old ills in mind and had but the faintest feelings of rancour.

5.24

　　子曰："孰谓微生高直¹？""或乞醯焉²，乞诸其邻而与之。

【中译文】

　　孔子说："谁说微生高这个人直爽？有人向他借点

論語意解

一　一

一　一

二　一

【注释】

1　陈：春秋时的古国，妫（guī）姓。商殷灭亡后，周武王找到了舜的后代妫满，封他于陈。其地约在今河南省东部（开封市以东）、安徽省北部（亳县以北）一带，故都在宛丘（今河南省淮阳县）。春秋末年，陈国被楚国所灭。

2　与：同"欤"。语气助词。

3　吾党：我的故乡（鲁国）。古代五百家为一党。狂简："狂"，指心气很高，志向远大；"简"，指简单粗率、意气用事。

4　斐然："斐（fěi）"，本义指五色错杂。形容有文采的样子。章：花纹，文采。引申为文学，文章。

5　裁：节制，控制。这里有"指导"的意思。此句，《史记·孔子世家》为"吾不知所以裁之"。由此推断，文中省略的主语应是"吾"。

【英译文】

　　When the Master was in Chen Slate he said, Let us go back, let us go back! The little ones at home are headstrong and careless. They are perfecting themselves in all the showy insignia of culture without any idea how to use them.

5.23

　　子曰："伯夷、叔齐不念旧恶¹，怨是用希²。"

官），乃楚左史倚相之后，与孔子同时或较早于孔子。相传左丘明曾为《春秋》作传（称为《左传》），又作《国语》（也有学者认为，《左传》和《国语》的作者并非一人，二书也并非左丘明所作）。又传说，左丘明是个瞎子，故有"左丘失明"之说。

2 匿：隐藏起来，不让人知道。

【英译文】

The Master (Confucius) said, Clever talk, a pretentious manner and a reverence that is only of the feet-Zuo Qiuming was incapable of stooping to them, and I too could never stoop to them. Having to conceal one's indignation and keep on friendly terms with the people against whom one feels it-Zuo Qiuming was incapable of stooping to such conduct, and I too am incapable of stooping to such conduct.

5.26

颜渊、季路侍[1]。子曰："盍各言尔志[2]？"子路曰："愿车马衣裘[3]，与朋友共，敝之而无憾。"颜渊曰："愿无伐善[4]，无施劳[5]。"子路曰："愿闻子之志。"子曰："老者安之，朋友信之，少者怀之。"

【中译文】

颜渊、子路在孔子身边。孔子说："何不说说你们各自的志向？"子路说："愿意把车马皮衣拿出来与朋

醋，他没直说没有，却到他的邻居家去借来给人了。"

【注释】

1 微生高：姓微生，名高。《庄子》、《战国策》中又称之为"尾生高"。鲁国人，以直爽守信而著称。

2 醯（xī）：醋。

【英译文】

The Master (Confucius) said, How can we call even Wei shenggao upright? When someone asked him for vinegar he begged it from the people next door, and then gave it as though it were his own gift.

5.25

子曰："巧言，令色，足恭，左丘明耻之[1]，丘亦耻之。匿怨而友其人[2]，左丘明耻之，丘亦耻之。"

【中译文】

孔子说："甜言蜜语，虚容假色，过分卑恭，对这种人，左丘明以为可耻，我孔丘也以为可耻。把怨恨隐藏在心里，却假装与人友好，对这种人，左丘明以为可耻，我孔丘也以为可耻。"

【注释】

1 左丘明：春秋时鲁国人，担任过鲁国的太史（朝廷史

【英译文】

The Master (Confucius) said, Clever talk, a pretentious manner and a reverence that is only of the feet—Zuo Qiuming was incapable of stooping to them, and I too could never stoop to them. Having to conceal one's indignation and keep on friendly terms with the people against whom one feels it—Zuo Qiuming was incapable of stooping to such conduct, and I too am incapable of stooping to such conduct.

5.26

子曰："巧言、令色、足恭，左丘明耻之，丘亦耻之。匿怨而友其人，左丘明耻之，丘亦耻之。"

【中译文】

【注释】

【英译文】

The Master (Confucius) said, How can we ever call even Wei shenggao upright? When someone asked him for vinegar, he begged it from the people next door, and then gave it as though it were his own gift.

5.25

子曰："孰谓微生高直？或乞醢焉，乞诸其邻而与之。"

【中译文】

【注释】

them; in dealing with friends, to be of good faith with them; in dealing with the young, to cherish them.

5.27
子曰："已矣乎[1]！吾未见能见其过而内自讼者也[2]。"

【中译文】
孔子说："罢了吧！我还没看到过能主动认识自己的错误而且能自觉地自我责备的人。"

【注释】
1 已：罢了，算了。下面的"矣""乎"，都是表示绝望的感叹助词。
2 讼(sòng)：责备，争辩是非。

【英译文】
The Master (Confucius) said, In vain have I met a single man capable of seeing his own faults and bringing the charge home against himself.

5.28
子曰："十室之邑[1]，必有忠信如丘者焉，不如丘之好学也。"

【中译文】
孔子说："在十户人家居住的小地方，也一定有象

论语意解

友共同享用，就是用坏了穿破旧了也没什么不满。"颜渊说："我愿意不夸耀自己的长处，不表白自己的功劳。"子路说："愿意听听老师您的志向。"孔子说："使老人安康舒适，使朋友互相信任，使孩子得到关怀爱护。"

【注释】
1 季路：即子路。因侍于季氏，又称季路。侍：服侍，陪从在尊长身边站着。《论语》中，单用"侍"字，指孔子坐着，弟子站着。用"侍坐"指孔子坐着，弟子也坐着。用"侍侧"，指弟子陪从孔子，或立或坐。
2 盍(hé)：何不。
3 裘(qiú)：皮衣。
4 伐：夸耀，自夸。
5 施：表白。一说，"施"，是施加给别人。句中"无施劳"，是不把劳苦的事加在别人身上，即自己不辞劳苦，对劳累的事不推脱。

【英译文】
Once when Yan Hui and Zi Lu were waiting upon him, the Master said, Suppose each of you were to tell his wish. Zi Lu said, I should like to have carriages and horsed, clothes and fur rugs, share them with my friends and feel no annoyance if they were returned to me the worse for wear. Yan Hui said, I should like never to boast of my good qualities nor make a fuss about the trouble I take on behalf of others. Zi Lu said, A thing I should like is to hear the Master's wish. The Master said, In dealing with the aged, to be of comfort to

解读论语

5.27

子曰："已矣乎！吾未见能见其过而内自讼者也。"

【中译文】

孔子说："算了吧！我还没看到能够主动检查自己的错误而且能自觉地自我责备的人。"

【注释】

1. 已：罢了，算了。下句即"矣"、"乎"，语气词，表强烈的感叹语调。
2. 讼(sòng)：责备，争辩是非。

【英译文】

The Master (Confucius) said, In vain have I met a single man capable of seeing his own faults and bringing the charge home against himself.

5.28

子曰："十室之邑，必有忠信如丘者焉，不如丘之好学也。"

【中译文】

孔子说："有十户人家居住的小地方，必定会有

像我这样讲忠信的人，但是比不上我那么好学不倦地追求美德。"子路说："愿意听听老师的志向。"孔子说："使老人安乐幸福，使朋友互相信任，使年轻子辈得到关怀爱护。"

【注释】

1. 季路：即子路。因排行下本行五，又称季路。伴：陪侍。随从在尊长身边跟随着。《论语》中，单用"侍"字，指闲立着；用"侍坐"指陪孔子坐着；用"侍侧"，指陪孔子身旁，或立或坐。
2. 盍(hé)：何不。
3. 忿(fèn)：夸大。
4. 伐：夸耀，自夸。
5. 施：一说"施"，是施加于别人。一说施读为"弛"，是不把劳苦的事加在别人身上。由自己承担劳苦，对劳累的事毫不推辞。

【英译文】

Once when Yan Hui and Zi Lu were waiting upon him, the Master said, Suppose each of you were to tell his wish. Zi Lu said, I should like to have carriages and horses, clothes and fur rugs, share them with my friends and feel no annoyance if they were returned to me the worse for wear. Yan Hui said, I should like never to boast of my good qualities nor make a fuss about the trouble I take on behalf of others. Zi Lu said, A thing I should like is to hear the Master's wish. The Master said, In dealing with the aged, to be of comfort to them; in dealing with friends, to be of good faith with them; in dealing with the young, to cherish them.

我这样讲究忠信的人，只是不如我这样喜欢学习罢了。"

【注释】

1 十室：十户人家。古时，九夫为井，四井为邑，一邑共有三十二户人家。"十室之邑"极言其小，是指尚且不满三十二家的小村邑。

【英译文】

The Master (Confucius) said, In an hamlet of ten houses you may be sure of finding someone who is quite as loyal and true to his word as I. But I doubt if you would find anyone who equals my love of learning.

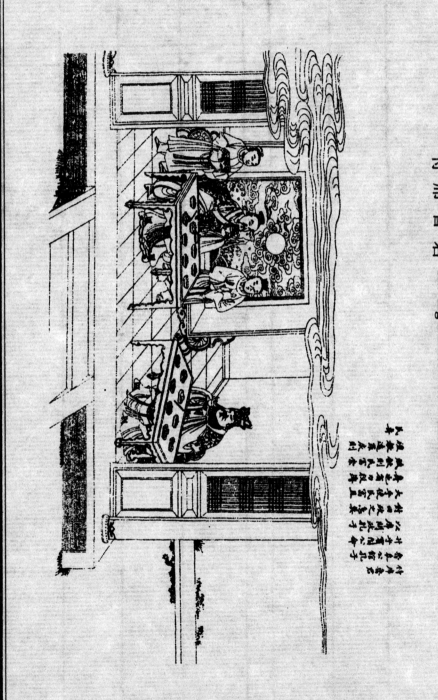

侍席鲁君 Having Dinner with Duke of State Lu

论语意解

论语意释

像这样有忠信品德的人，只是不如我这样喜欢学习罢了。"

【注释】

1. 十室：十户人家。古制，九夫为井，四井为邑，一邑共有三十六户人家。"十室之邑"极言其小，是指尚且不满三十二家的小村邑。

【英译文】

The Master (Confucius) said, in an hamlet of ten houses you may be sure of finding someone who is quite as loyal and true to his word as I. But I doubt if you would find anyone who equals my love of learning.

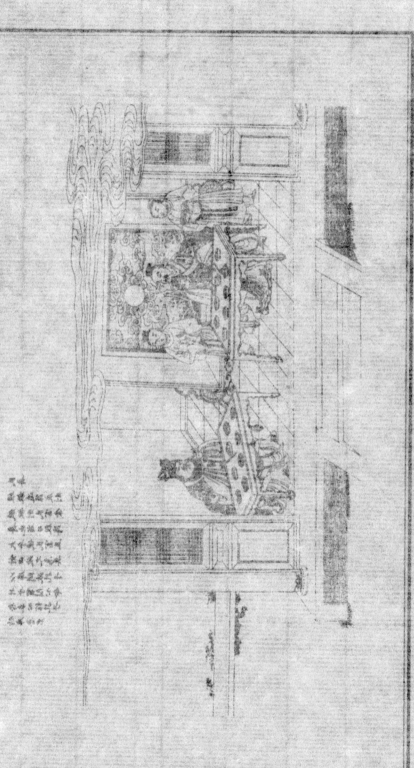

【中译文】

仲弓问子桑伯子这个人怎么样。孔子说："还可以，办事简要。"仲弓说："态度严肃认真，又办事简要，用这样的方式去对待人民，不也是可以的吗？但是为人简便，办事又简易粗率，岂不是太简单化了吗？"孔子说："冉雍，你的话很对。"

【注释】

1 仲弓：就是冉雍。子桑伯子：人名。其身世情况不详。有的学者认为，子桑伯子是鲁国人，即《庄子》中所说子桑户"，与"琴张"为友。又有人以为是秦穆公时的"子桑"（公孙枝）。但皆无确考。

2 简：简单，简约，不烦琐。

3 居：平时的做人，为人，居心。

4 临：面对，面临。这里含有治理的意思。

5 无乃：岂不是，难道不是。大：同"太"。

【英译文】

When Zhong Gong asked about Zisang Bozi, the Master said, he is adequate but simple. Zhong Gong said, I can understand that such a man might do as a ruler, provided he were scrupulous in his own conduct and lax only in his dealings with the people. But you would admit that a man who was lax in his own conduct as well as in government would be too lax. The Master said, What you says is quite true.

论语意解

一一〇 一一九

雍也篇第六 （共三十章）

What Confucius and His Students said

6.1

子曰："雍也，可使南面[1]。"

【中译文】

孔子说："冉雍这个人，可以让他主政一方。"

【注释】

1 南面：就是脸朝南。古代以坐北朝南为尊位、正位。从君王、诸侯、将、相到地方军政长官，坐堂听政，都是面南而坐。这里指主政一方。

【英译文】

The Master (Confucius) said, Ran Yong might be set in a position as a high-ranked official.

6.2

仲弓问子桑伯子[1]。子曰："可也，简[2]。"仲弓曰："居敬而行简[3]，以临其民[4]，不亦可乎？居简而行简，无乃大简乎[5]？"子曰："雍之言然。"

六本篇第十五 （卷第三十）

What Confucius and His Students said

6.1

【文结中】

子曰："嚣嚣，口乎。"

【注释】

一无所能以为乎，八个有能者乎，说子之言。

【文结义】

W君，致其殊皆不知能得，经，容聚，王君乎
说无恶，具未知遂先师临摄，学聆谢临省来
四，致则故辈临识临得成。

6.2

孔子言之，曰："何用其德代之乎？"曰："君
子德贵之乎，行何必知乎乎？"曰："何用圣之乎
中。"曰："遂。"

The Master (Confucius) said, Ran You, your might be set in a position as a right-mindedness.

【文结义】

When Zhong Gong asked about Zizhang Bo Zi, the Master said, I can understand that such a man might be ap-

【注释】

1 中由：孔子的弟子，姓仲名由，字子路。
2 周：周密，周到。周周；周围。
3 周：少周，少犯。人：人的情况的不足。
4 嚣：嚣嚣的样子恼其名者重复。周密：周到。
5 王子：周。乎大容浪，然不乎，代之乎。

【文结义】

When Zhong Gong asked about Zizhang Bo Zi, the Master said, I can understand that such a man might be ap-
probed, but simple, that is, Zizhang Bo Zi and his conduct were scrupulous in his own conduct and behaved simply to be op-
do as a man who was two men who would plow with the people. During plow limbs that a man was two in his
his dealings with the people. But plow, too, he be noot be too unkind as well as Zizhang Bo Zi, too lax. The Master said,
What you says is quite true.

6.4

　　子华使于齐[1]，冉子为其母请粟[2]。子曰："与之釜[3]。"请益[4]。曰："与之庾[5]。"冉子与之粟五秉[6]。子曰："赤之适齐也[7]，乘肥马，衣轻裘[8]。吾闻之也，君子周急不继富[9]。"

【中译文】

　　子华出使去齐国，冉求替子华的母亲请求给些小米。孔子说："给他六斗四升。"冉求请求再增加些。孔子说："再给他二斗四升。"冉求却给了他小米八十石。孔子说："子华到齐国去，乘坐肥马驾的车，身穿又轻又暖的皮衣。我听说过，君子应周济急需帮助的人，而不要使富人更富。"

【注释】

1 子华：即公西赤。
2 冉子：即冉求。粟：谷子，小米。
3 釜（fǔ）：古代容量名。一釜当时合六斗四升。古代的斗小，一斗约合现在二升，一釜约等于现在一斗二升八合。一釜粮食仅是一个人一月的口粮。
4 益：增添，增加。
5 庾（yǔ）：古代容量名。一庾合当时二斗四升，约合现在四升八合。一说，一庾当时合十六斗，约合现在三斗二升。
6 秉（bǐng）：古代容量名。一秉合十六斛，一斛合十

论语意解

6.3

　　哀公问："弟子孰为好学？"孔子对曰："有颜回者好学，不迁怒[1]，不贰过[2]。不幸短命死矣。今也则亡[3]，未闻好学者也。"

【中译文】

　　鲁哀公问孔子："你的学生中谁是爱好学习的呢？"孔子回答："有一个叫颜回的，很好学，他从来不迁怒于他人，不犯同样的错误。但不幸的是他短命死了。现在就没有那样的人了，没听到有好学的人了。"

【注释】

1 迁怒：指自己不如意时，对别人发火生气；或受了甲的气，却转移目标，拿乙去出气。"迁"，转移。
2 贰：二，再一次，重复。
3 亡：同"无"。

【英译文】

　　Duke Ai asked which of the disciples had a love of learning. The Master answered him, There was Yan Hui. He had a great love of learning. He never vented his wrath upon the innocent nor let others suffer for his faults. Unfortunately the span of life allotted to him by Heaven was short, and he died. At present there is no one like him. I have heard of none who are fond of learning.

6.4

子华使于齐[1]，冉子为其母请粟[2]。子曰："与之釜[3]。"请益[4]。曰："与之庾[5]。"冉子与之粟五秉[6]。子曰："赤之适齐也，乘肥马，衣轻裘。吾闻之也，君子周急不继富[8]。"

【中译文】

子华出使去齐国，冉有替子华的母亲来请给些小米。孔子说："给她六斗四升。"冉有请求再增加。孔子说："再给她二斗四升。"冉有却给了他八十斛。孔子说："公西赤到齐国去，乘坐肥壮的骡马，身穿又轻又暖的皮袍。我听说过，君子只周济急需帮助的人，而不是使富人更富。"

【注释】

1 子华：即公西赤。

2 冉子：即冉求。粟：谷子，小米。

3 釜(fǔ)：古代容量名。一釜约当时合六斗四升。古代的斗小，一斗约合现在三升，一釜约等于现在一斗二升八合。一釜换算成现是一个人一月的口粮。

4 益：增添，增加。

5 庾(yǔ)：古代容量名。一庾约当时二斗四升，约合现在四升八合。一说，一庾当时合十六斗，约合现在三斗二升。

6 秉(bǐng)：古代容量名。一秉合十六斛，一斛合十……

6.3

哀公问："弟子孰为好学？"孔子对曰："有颜回者好学，不迁怒[1]，不贰过[2]。不幸短命死矣，今也则亡[3]，未闻好学者也。"

【中译文】

鲁哀公问孔子："你的学生中谁是爱好学习的呢？"孔子回答："有一个叫颜回的，很好学，他从来不迁怒于他人，不犯同样的错误。可惜他短命死了，现在就没有那样的人了，没听到好学的人了。"

【注释】

1 迁怒：指自己不如意时，对别人发火生气；迁：转移。

2 贰：再一次，重复。

3 亡：同"无"。

【英译文】

Duke Ai asked which of the disciples had a love of learning. The Master answered him, "There was Yan Hui. He had a great love of learning. He never vented his wrath upon the innocent nor let others suffer for his faults. Unfortunately the span of life allotted to him by Heaven was short, and he died. At present there is no one like him. I have heard of none who are fond of learning."

人（一说，宋国人）。生于公元前 515 年，卒年不详。孔子在鲁国任司寇（司法官员）时，原思在孔子家做过总管（家臣）。孔子死后，原思退隐，居卫国。之：指代孔子。

2 之：代指原思。九百：九百斗。一说，指九百斛，则是九百石，不可确考。

3 毋：不要，勿。

4 邻里乡党：古代以五家为邻，二十五家为里，五百家为党，一万二千五百家为乡。这里泛指原思家乡的人们。

【英译文】

When Yuan Si was made a governor, he was given an allowance of nine hundred measures of grain, but declined it. The Master said, Surely you could find people who would be glad of it among your neighbours or villagers.

6.6

子谓仲弓，曰："犁牛之子骍且角[1]，虽欲勿用，山川其舍诸[2]？"

【中译文】

孔子谈论仲弓，说："耕牛生的一个小牛犊，长着整齐的红毛和周正的硬角，虽然不想用它，山川之神都不会舍弃它呢？"

斗。"五秉"，就是八百斗（八十石）。约合现在十六石。

7 适：往，去。

8 衣（yì）：穿。

9 周：周济，救济。继：接济，增益。

【英译文】

When Zi Hua was sent on a mission to Qi State, Ran You asked that Hua's mother might be granted an allowance of grain, The Master said, Give her a cauldron full. Ran said that was not enough. The Master said, Give her a measure. Ran gave her five bundles. The Master said, When Zi Hua went to Qi he drove sleek horses and was wrapped in light furs. There is a saying, A gentleman helps out the needy; he does not make the rich richer still.

6.5

原思为之宰[1]，与之粟九百[2]，辞。子曰："毋[3]！以与尔邻里乡党乎[4]！"

【中译文】

原思在孔子家做总管，孔子给他九百斗小米，原思推辞不要。孔子说："不要推辞！可以分给你家乡的邻里乡亲嘛！"

【注释】

1 原思：孔子的弟子。姓原，名宪，字子思。鲁国

论语意解

论语意解

人（一说，宋国人）。生于公元前515年，卒年不详。孔子在鲁国任司寇（司法官员）时，原思在孔子家做过总管（家臣）。孔子死后，原思退隐，居卫国，之后代孔子。

2 之：代指原思。九百，九百斗。一句，指九百斛（即九百石，不可确考）。

3 毋：不要。以，则。

4 邻里乡党：古代以五家为邻，二十五家为里，五百家为党，一万二千五百家为乡。这里泛指周围家乡的人们。

【英译文】

When Yuan Si was made a governor, he was given an allowance of nine hundred measures of grain, but declined it. The Master said, Surely you could find people who would be glad of it among your neighbours or villagers.

6.6

子谓仲弓，曰："犁牛之子骍且角，虽欲勿用，山川其舍诸？"

【中译文】

孔子谈论仲弓，说："耕牛生的一个小牛犊，长着整齐的红毛和周正的犄角，虽然不想用它，山川之神难道会舍弃它呢？"

【注释】

1 原思：孔子的弟子。姓原，名宪，字子思。鲁国 人。"一说"，"禄是八百斗（八十石）"。"钧合现在十六石。

2 适：往。

3 衣（yì）：穿。

9 周：周济。殷实，较穷。增益。

【英译文】

When Zi Hua was sent on a mission to Qi State, Ran You asked that Hua's mother might be granted an allowance of grain. The Master said, Give her a cauldron full. Ran said that was not enough. The Master said, Give her a measure. Ran gave her five bundles. The Master said, When Zi Hua went to Qi he drove sleek horses and was wrapped in light furs. There is a saying, A gentleman helps out the needy; he does not make the rich richer still.

6.5

原思为之宰，与之粟九百，辞。子曰："毋！以与尔邻里乡党乎！"

了。"

【注释】

1 三月：不是具体指三个月，而是泛指较长的时间。
2 日月：一天，一月。泛指较短的时间，偶尔。至：达到，做到。

【英译文】

The Master (Confucius) said, Yan Hui is capable of occupying his whole mind for three months on end with no thought but that of Goodness. The others can do so only for a short time.

6.8

季康子问[1]："仲由可使从政也与？"子曰："由也果，于从政乎何有[2]？"曰："赐也可使从政也与？"曰："赐也达，于从政乎何有？"曰："求也可使从政也与？"曰："求也艺，于从政乎何有？"

【中译文】

季康子问："仲由，可以让他做官从政吗？"孔子说："仲由果断勇敢，从政有什么困难呢？"季康子说："子贡，可以让他做官从政吗？"孔子说："子贡通达事理，对于从政有什么困难呢？"季康子说："冉求，可以让他做官从政吗？"孔子说："冉求，多才多艺，

【注释】

1 "犁牛"句："犁牛"，杂色的耕牛。"子"，指小牛犊。"骍"，赤色牛。周代崇尚赤色，祭祀用的牛，要求是长着红毛和端正的长角的牛，不能用普通的耕牛来代替。这里用"犁牛之子"，比喻冉雍（仲弓）。据说冉雍的父亲是失去贵族身份的"贱人"，品行也不好。孔子认为，冉雍德行才学都好，子能改父之过，变恶以为美，是可以做大官的（当时冉雍担任季氏的家臣）。
2 山川：指山川之神。这里比喻君主或贵族统治者。其：表示反问的语助词。怎么会，难道，哪能。舍：舍弃，不用。

【英译文】

The Master (Confucius) said of Zhong Gong, If the offspring of a brindled ox is ruddy-coated and has grown its horns, however much people might hesitate to use it, would the hills and streams really reject it?

6.7

子曰："回也，其心三月不违仁[1]，其馀则日月至焉而已矣[2]。"

【中译文】

孔子说："颜回这个人，可以在长时间内不违背仁德，其馀的弟子们只能在短时间内偶尔做到仁德罢

论语意译

【注释】（6.6）

1 "犁牛"句："犁牛"，杂色的耕牛。"子"，指小牛犊。"骍"，赤色。周代崇尚赤色，祭祀用的牛要毛色纯正，毛和端正的长角的牛，不能用普通的耕牛来代替。这里用"犁牛之子"，比喻仲弓虽然由地位父亲微贱家庭的"贱人"，品行也不好，孔子认为，仲弓德行才学很好，主张改为父之子，变惩以其美，是可以做大官的（当时由举荐得进用孝廉家臣）。

2 山川：指山川之神。这里比喻杰出才德贤能治者。
其：表示反问的语气，怎么会，难道。诸：兼词，相当"之乎"。
舍：不用。

【英译文】（6.6）

The Master (Confucius) said of Zhong Gong, If the offspring of a brindled ox is ruddy-coated and has grown its horns, however much people might hesitate to use it, would the hills and streams really reject it?

6.7

子曰："回也，其心三月不违仁，其余则日月至焉而已矣。"

【中译文】（6.7）

孔子说："颜回这个人，……其余的弟子们只能在短时间内偶尔做到不违背仁德……"

【注释】（6.7）

1 三月：不是具体指三个月，而是泛指较长的时间。

2 日月：一天、一月。泛指较短的时间。焉：于是，从这里。指到，做到。

【英译文】（6.7）

The Master (Confucius) said, Yan Hui is capable of occupying his whole mind for three months on end with no thought but that of Goodness. The others can do so only for a short time.

6.8

季康子问："仲由可使从政也与？"子曰："由也果，于从政乎何有？"曰："赐也可使从政也与？"曰："赐也达，于从政乎何有？"曰："求也可使从政也与？"曰："求也艺，于从政乎何有？"

【中译文】（6.8）

季康子问："仲由，可以让他治理政事吗？"孔子说："仲由果断敢决，从政有什么困难呢？"季康子说："端木赐，可以让他治理政事吗？"孔子说："子贡通达事理，治理政事有什么困难呢？"季康子说："冉求，可以让他治理政事吗？"孔子说："冉求多才多艺……"